Chicken Bucks

Also by Susan Sharpe

Waterman's Boy
Spirit Quest

Chicken Bucks

by Susan Sharpe

Bradbury Press New York

Maxwell Macmillan Canada Toronto
Maxwell Macmillan International
New York Oxford Singapore Sydney

Bradbury Press
Macmillan Publishing Company
866 Third Avenue
New York, NY 10022

Maxwell Macmillan Canada, Inc.
1200 Eglinton Avenue East
Suite 200
Don Mills, Ontario M3C 3N1

Macmillan Publishing Company is part of the Maxwell Communication Group of Companies.

First edition
Printed and bound in the United States of America
10 9 8 7 6 5 4 3 2 1

Library of Congress Cataloging-in-Publication Data
Sharpe, Susan.
Chicken bucks / by Susan Sharpe. — 1st ed.
p.   cm.
Summary: When hard times force twelve-year-old Mark to change his
4-H project from raising a calf to selling eggs from his chickens,
he finds that the experience is both challenging and surprisingly rewarding.
ISBN 0-02-782353-9
[1. Farm life—Fiction. 2. Chickens—Fiction. 3. Moneymaking
projects—Fiction.] I. Title.
PZ7.S5323Ch 1992
[Fic]—dc20   92-5049

To Kathy Courrier

Thanks to many farmers in Minnesota and Iowa who graciously shared their knowledge with me, including Dwight Ault, Susan Bayh, Jacob Courrier, Margaret and Orville Courrier, Bathsheba Demuth, Chris Frantsvog, David and Amy Kenis, Cindy and Gerald Mattson, Susan Monson, Roger Nelson, and Ann Robinson. And for very different but also invaluable guidance, thanks to Sharon Steinhoff.

1

. . . .

April rain. Mark Swenson shivered inside his poncho as he waited for the school bus, raindrops loud on the top of his hood. The last of the dirty old snow had melted away, and now the water in the ditch beside the road was brown with topsoil washed out of the field.

Rain made the planting late. It was time to start the corn, but the fields were too wet; the big tractors would sink in the mud. Jessica was late, too. She was writing a poem about rain. He had left her standing at the kitchen table in her raincoat, printing furiously. She'd better get here. Mom had already gone into town for her day at the newspaper, so Mark was responsible.

He peered down the straight, flat road. He would see the bus when it came over a little rise, about a half mile away. On each side of the road the sand-colored stubble of last year's corn waited to be turned under before the new planting.

Mark loved planting time; his parents were always cheerful and hopeful, and the fields would be cleaned off to the beautiful, bare, blue-black soil. Best of all, Mark was allowed to drive the tractor now. Not the big tractor, of course, but the little Farmall. He had just turned twelve.

Honk! The school bus door whooshed open, and there sat the bus driver, Mitch Harl, smiling at him.

"Jessica's late," Mark began to explain, but Mitch pointed beyond him. There she came, glasses joggling on her freckled nose, boots kicking up mud, wet poem clutched in her hand.

Mark hopped over the ditch and climbed up the steps into the warm, dry bus. Jessica sat near the back, where she could mutter poetry out loud and no one cared. Mark liked to sit by a window to see how the farms were doing.

First came the Halvorsens', and then the Fogelman farm. The Fogelmans had owned their land forever, even longer than the Swensons or the Halvorsens. But the Fogelmans were kind of odd; you could tell the grown-ups thought so, even though they said nice things out loud. The Fogelmans were always trying different animals and new crops or new ways of planting. They even had a llama. Mark often saw it, huddled up against the barn, its silly long neck raised up to look at the bus.

Whoosh! The door opened, and Emma Halvorsen's face, edged with long blond hair, appeared above the steps.

"Where's your little sister?" asked Mitch.

"She's got a cold."

Mitch shook his head sympathetically. "Keep her out of this rain."

Emma hesitated a moment in the aisle. Usually she sat beside her sister, who was even younger than Jessica, only a first grader. But today, when Mark glanced at her, she sat beside him.

"Hi," she said.

"Hi."

Mark didn't know what to say. He liked Emma, who was in his class. She was a good sister to little Lisa. And she didn't let other kids bother her, like the day Stevie Johnson said her name sounded like a disgusting word, and Emma answered him right back. She said it was her grandmother's name, and she guessed she had a right to it. Mark admired her for that.

"Are you going to 4-H on Thursday?" Emma asked.

"Sure." Mark hardly ever missed 4-H.

"You going to show anything at the fair this year?"

"Yeah." Mark looked out the window; they were almost at the river. "My dad's going to buy me a calf, maybe even this weekend. Uncle Robert is taking me to the big sale barn in Rochester. He's taking me and my cousins, Bobby and Jerry. They already got calves, for Christmas. But he said he'd help me pick out a good one."

"You'd like to beat your cousins, wouldn't you?"

"Not really." Mark looked sideways at Emma. He did want to beat out his Nelson cousins, of course. For three years now Bobby and Jerry had shown their cattle at the county fair in August, and each year one of them had won a ribbon. Mark would show a hog that his father had given him. He had never won anything.

"What about you?" Mark asked Emma. "You going to enter the fair this year?"

"I guess so," she replied indifferently.

"You got a calf?" Mark had never heard her talk about her 4-H project, though she usually came to the meetings.

"No," she answered.

"What are you going to enter, then?"

"Flowers," she said.

Mark stared at her, and then he started to laugh. "You can't grow flowers for 4-H!"

4

"Why not?"

For a kid who had grown up in southern Minnesota, right here near the Iowa border, Emma sure didn't know much about farming, Mark thought. But he tried to be nice.

"Because, you know, 4-H is for farm projects. The stuff that farmers raise. Some people grow vegetables, I guess. But don't you think that would be kind of boring? You could raise a calf; it's not that hard. Your dad could give you one, and keep it with his."

"Yes, but I want to do something more on my own. Without his help."

"Yeah, that's just like me," Mark agreed. "My dad has hogs, so I don't want to raise a hog this time. But you could raise one, Emma. Hogs bring good money, my dad says so."

"A hog would be all right," said Emma politely but firmly, "but I'm going to grow flowers."

There was obviously no use talking to her. He wondered what their 4-H leader, Thelma Olson, was going to say about it. Anyway, he had missed seeing the last farm, and now they were at school.

Whoosh! As the door of the bus opened, children stampeded out. The rain had let up to a quiet dampness. Mark watched to make sure Jessica made it into the third-grade room. She could get awfully dreamy when she was writing.

Jerry Nelson was hanging up his coat at the lockers

with his brother, Bobby, who was one year older, in the seventh grade across the hall. The seventh grade used to be in the junior high school, but since there were fewer children now, the seventh grade had been moved right in here. The junior high was closed, so everybody in 8 to 12 went to the high school. There were fewer children because some families had lost their farms. But Mark's cousins didn't have to worry. Their father had the biggest farm in the county, over a thousand acres.

"Jerry got kicked last night," Bobby greeted Mark. "He was messing with the steers. Dad told him he should know better."

Jerry pulled up the leg of his jeans to show an ugly black-and-blue all over his shin. But he didn't seem sorry. "It was my own," he said proudly. "He's a nasty one. But I'm going to tame him. I'm going to get him so I can lead him right around the ring at the fair, like a little calf."

"He's out there combing him so much, Dad says he's running a beauty parlor for steers," Bobby giggled.

Mark smiled. He had seen Jerry's steer; it was a fine red Hereford. "What you feeding him?" he asked, meaning to sound like a real farmer.

"What do you think I'm feeding him? Fried rutabagas? Corn and hay, stupid," Jerry answered sarcastically.

6

While Mrs. Sutter was calling everybody to their seats, Mark sat down to a pleasant daydream. He was showing his steer, he was standing before the 4-H judge, he could smell the animals and the hay, the popcorn and cotton candy. Jerry's steer was asked to leave the ring because it behaved so badly. Now the judge was holding up a blue ribbon. He would fasten it right to the rope halter that held the steer, and Mark would take one last walk around, while the people clapped. He saw his mother in the crowd, cheering, and his father, and Jessica. He even saw Emma, holding Lisa up to look at him.

He was supposed to be learning the names of the countries in the Middle East, but it was hard to concentrate. They all sounded the same. Iraq, Iran, what was the difference? And they were hard to spell. Qatar. How come they didn't put a *u* after the *q*, like they were supposed to?

"Where is Bahrain?" asked Mrs. Sutter. Emma had her hand up, but Mark couldn't remember.

The rain had stopped by the time Mark's bus reached his driveway, and the rivers of the morning had slowed to tiny trickles. It would be muddy everywhere now. Mark went into the kitchen to get a snack for Jessica and himself; his mother was still at the paper, and his father had gone to the bank today. Only Oscar greeted them, clicking his old toenails on the linoleum.

Mark tossed him a dog biscuit before he changed into his farm jeans and pulled on his rubber boots, ready to do his chores.

Mark did not mind doing farm chores. Jessica liked to help at the newspaper, but Mark preferred the farm. He loved to go outdoors in all kinds of weather—on a day like this, for instance, when the world smelled of change. If you looked up, you could see the gray clouds all in an uproar, masses of them moving up and around. There must be a big wind blowing up there. Yes, it had already blown out one tiny spot of blue sky, over above the old maple near the barn, and if you looked hard, it seemed as if the maple buds were fatter than a week ago, and redder. Soon it would clear up, soon another batch of pigs would be coming along, soon the tractors would be seen for acres around, like toys in the huge dark fields. The farm was always changing, but always the same, too.

Mark sniffed as he ambled toward the barn, his black rubber boots squishing in the black mud. It didn't smell of change, it smelled of hogs. The farm always smelled of hogs; but in April, when the manure piles began to get warm, it smelled especially of hogs.

When he came around the base of the big silver storage bin that still held some of last year's huge corn crop, Mark stepped up to a jog. His father's truck was there; good—he must be back home. That meant he would help with the evening chores.

His father was standing by the farrowing pen. He nodded briefly at Mark, who counted five piglets already lying on the clean hay. The sow was lying on her side, grunting and panting, and licking the wetness from her babies, when she could reach them.

The farrowing pen was a narrow metal cage. The bars at one end were lifted enough to let the piglets squirm in and out to nurse, but the sow could hardly move. It was necessary because otherwise a sow could roll over onto her babies and crush them.

"Get her a drink of water," Mr. Swenson said to Mark.

Mark ran into the equipment area to find a clean bucket, which was heavy when he had filled it at the tap. It bumped against his leg, and the water sloshed over a bit. Back at the pen, there was another piglet on the hay.

"How many more, Dad?"

"Maybe one, maybe two." He shook his head. "These are small. Some of them may not make it." The sow grunted again, a noise that sounded like a question, as if the sow herself did not understand what was happening. The piglets who had been born were already looking for a place to nurse. They rooted around in circles, sucking on anything their noses hit. Mr. Swenson had to remove several from his pants leg. One wandered all the way up around the sow's head and started sucking on her ear, until Mark reached in and moved it to a spot in front of a teat to nurse.

"Will she be able to feed them all?" Sometimes there were more piglets than nipples, or the sow did not have enough milk, and Mark and his mother and dad would take turns feeding the extra ones formula out of a bottle.

"Looks like," said Mr. Swenson. The sow kicked, trying to get up. "Easy, girl. Easy, now. Soooooo, pig, pig, pig." A shape appeared between the sow's hind legs, and then the piglet slipped out, covered with a film of thick wetness streaked with blood. The sow grunted and squirmed as Mr. Swenson set the new piglet by her nose where she could snuffle and lick it. Mark looked away.

"We could wash the piglets, Dad," he suggested.

His father laughed. "Get used to it, Mark. It's good for the sow. She licks that stuff off and she gives good colostrum. They'll need it, these little suckers. Keep them healthy. These are her piglets for now, and she knows the best thing to do."

The sow had laid her head back on the floor, breathing hard. The piglets wriggled and squirmed, already fighting over the best nipples, except for one that had fallen asleep. Mr. Swenson felt carefully along the sow's sides. "I guess that's it," he said. "Seven. Not bad, for her first birthing. We'll notch their ears on Saturday. Soooooo, pig, pig, pig. Good girl." He petted the sow some more, but she seemed to be asleep already. "What's the weather report for tonight?" he asked, standing and removing the gloves.

"I don't know."

"How am I going to make you a farmer if you don't know the weather report, day and night? We need a clear spell, so we can get moving on the planting. You check the other pigs already?"

"Not yet."

Mr. Swenson walked through the hog shed now, with one hand on Mark's shoulder, which was unusual. For some reason, it made Mark think about his 4-H project.

"Dad, I decided not to raise a pig for my 4-H this year. Do you mind? I just wanted to try something different. I want to raise a calf."

Mr. Swenson leaned over the side of the next pen, where the animals ranged from eighty to one hundred pounds. He just stood there, looking, not saying anything, which gave the boy an odd feeling. And then, instead of answering Mark, he started talking about the pigs again. "See that small one, over there? The gilt? She's got a red spot on her left frong leg. See it?"

The hogs moved about quickly, and were so crowded

11

in that it was hard to tell one from another. But at last Mark did see the spot, a nasty red sore on the inside of the leg.

"Somebody bit her, couple days ago," his father explained. "Got to keep an eye on it. If it gets puffy, we have to dose it with antibiotic. Understand?"

Mark shrank away from his father, because the words had a fierce sound. "Sure, Dad." He moved away, going about his chores with a strange feeling that things that seemed all right were not all right. He went outside and shoveled grain into the automatic feeder. He put fresh hay in the stall where the new piglets were. But when he got back, his father was still standing there, looking at the three-month pigs.

"The hogs okay?" Mark asked.

His father was slow in answering. "Mark, we've got trouble. I might as well tell you. I've already called your mother."

Mark waited, unable to guess.

"As you know, Mark, I went to the bank today. To pick up the loan money for spring planting, like we always do. But I only had half the mortgage payment to give them." He sighed. "I can give them the whole thing as soon as I sell this lot of hogs."

Mark nodded solemnly, but he didn't really understand. Maybe this was just some adult kind of trouble. His father thought he knew what a mortgage was, but it didn't make sense. How could you have to pay the bank if you already owned something?

But his father didn't look as if he was in an explaining mood. His father looked sad, which frightened Mark. "You see, land values have plummeted since we bought that extra three hundred acres three years ago. And now it's worth less than what I borrowed to buy it. We're in the same fix as all the other farmers you hear about."

Mark felt queasy. "You mean the farmers that sold out? The ones that left?"

His father shrugged. "Maybe not quite that bad. But there's no loan money for us this spring. How do they think I can pay off if I can't get my crop in the ground?" Now he sounded angry.

"You mean we can't *plant* this spring?"

"Well, they've got their job, at the bank, and I've got mine. But I'm going to sell a lot of hogs this week, because I've got to have cash for seed." He seemed to be talking to himself. "This is a good lot of hogs here, that'll cover the mortgage and the seed. But I'll still owe for anhydrous. How am I going to raise that?" He shook his head. "Could be we could go without fertilizer, one year. Herbicide, too. The fields are in good shape. I don't exactly know."

"But we had a good crop last year, Dad. We had the best corn yield around. You said so."

"I know, I know it, son. That's not the point. Trouble in the Middle East, and the price of oil goes up. Price of oil is practically the same thing as the price of fertilizer. Not to mention the fuel for the machines. The Steiger takes one hundred gallons every time I fill her up. The Deere is bad enough. I hoped to get a new head for the combine this year, too. Well, kiss that idea good-bye."

It didn't make any sense. How could they be in trouble, farming along the way they had always done? In a way, Mark did not believe it. Someone at the bank must have made a mistake.

"We're studying the Middle East in school," he said, hoping maybe his father needed to think about something else for a while.

"Well, good for you. I guess maybe Minnesota and Teheran are a lot closer than they used to be, eh?"

"No, of course not. How could they get closer?"

Mr. Swenson smiled at last. "Well, then I guess we'll just have to work out our own solutions right here in the Midwest."

"I guess so. And Dad? Bobby said Uncle Robert is going to take them to the auction in Rochester on Saturday, and I can go with them. Is that okay? And I need money for the calf, you know, for 4-H. He says they've gone up a lot. Last year they were going for seventy-five cents a pound, but this year it's more like a dollar."

Charlie Swenson swung around suddenly, fiercely, looking at Mark. "You're asking me, right now, to buy you a five-hundred-dollar calf?"

"Well, you know, I could get a smaller one. Size isn't everything at the fair. I guess I'd still have a chance to fatten him up real good, before August. But it's already late to be getting one, Dad."

Mr. Swenson had turned his face away from his son. "Mark, listen. You're not understanding me. It's true you've been a great help on the farm recently. That's what a twelve-year-old ought to do. But it doesn't begin to pay for corn to fatten a calf. And then I suppose you'd want fencing, to give him a yard, and there are veterinary costs. No, Mark. We can't make a profit on one calf, and I don't have the money for pets."

"Sure, Dad." Mark wanted to cry. "I understand. It's not important. It's only 4-H. I don't mind." Mark whirled around out of the hog shed before his father could say any more. He ran fast, picking the heavy rubber boots up out of the mud, but he ran away from the house and up into the cornfield, where the stubble of the wonderful corn crop stood in raggedy brown rows. What sense did it make, what good did it do to be a good farmer, if a bank could take it all away from you?

He reached the top of the hill; not a high hill, but high enough to give a view of the landscape around, the straight road that went into town, the patchwork rolls of the Fogelman farm, and beyond them the river with its line of brushy, bare trees. How could the Fogelmans be making money? They had the hilliest farm, which Mr. Fogelman plowed along the curves of the hills and planted to alfalfa, oats, and something called amaranth, along with the corn. The Fogelman farm looked like some crazy-quilt pattern. In the other direction, his father's land lay in smooth, flat, straight corn rows, and beyond them were the new three hundred acres, the flattest land of all, the best for corn. Mark remembered when his parents had bought it, how lucky they'd felt. Corn brought the most money. Mark had believed that the new land would make them rich, and now his father was talking about losing the farm.

That couldn't be right, could it? Mark felt heavy. It could be right. So many families were gone. That kid who used to play the harmonica was gone. The people who had sold them the new acres were gone. The whole junior high was closed. His mother had started a new column in the paper called "Faraway Friends," with all the birth and death and wedding notes that came in from Rochester or Des Moines or the Twin Cities.

Mark looked over toward the Fogelmans' again. The sheep were leaving the shelter of the barn, coming out to pasture. A bit of sun shot through the clouds now, and lit up the flock, standing facing into the light. A thin whining noise was Mr. Fogelman bringing a load of hay out to the field with the tractor.

And then Mark did cry. Because it did matter! It mattered about his calf, about his 4-H project. He thought about Bobby and Jerry there at the auction, without him. Maybe he would never go back to 4-H again.

2

·······

"Hey, Dad, would you like to hear my poem about rain?" It was Thursday supper, and Mark had skipped 4-H. Charlie Swenson had been in a bad temper for three days. He agreed to hear Jessica's poem, but not very enthusiastically.

" 'Rain,' " she began, putting her fork down.

"You shouldn't say poetry with your mouth full," Mark reminded her.

"Mark, let it go," said Mrs. Swenson, who was always "Addy" in the family, short for Adelaide. "Now, Jess, let's hear it."

" 'Rain,' " she started again. " 'Rain is lovely, rain is fine, rain is raining all the time.' "

"Very nice," Addy said.

"Do you think it's good enough to put in the paper?" Jessica asked hopefully. Ever since her poem about hogs had won the grade-school prize and been published, she thought everything she wrote should be published. Or so it seemed to Mark.

"The poem's dumb," he objected. "The rain isn't fine; it's getting in the way of planting." He looked across at his father, who was picking at the roast on his plate, not bringing any to his mouth.

"It has good rhythm, Jess," said Addy gently. "But we don't have room for poetry this week. Too much bad business news to print." She, too, glanced over at Charlie. "Mark is right, rain has delayed the planting." She kept clutching her napkin tightly and then letting it go; the paper was all crinkled in tight lines, like the skin on the back of Grandma's hand.

"I thought we weren't even going to plant this spring," said Mark bitterly.

"We're going to plant, Mark." Mr. Swenson looked up at his wife, and Mark could tell they had agreed about something. "Only we're going to do it differently. I'm going to spread the whole manure pile on the fields. No anhydrous this year. And no weed killers, either. We're just going to cultivate to control

19

weeds, if I can figure a way to do it without eroding the topsoil. I've already talked to the Extension Service. And we're going to go have a look at Fogelman's operation."

Fogelman! Mark's fork clattered onto the floor. "What are you going there for?"

"Because Fogelman's making money."

"But he's weird, Dad. Everyone knows he's weird. He plants his land weird, with the weeds still in it." Mark leaned over to pick up his fork.

"Mark," said his mother, "we don't call people weird. And Mark, I want you to be very clear about one thing." She looked hard at her husband. "This is a grown-up problem. This has nothing to do with you. Your father and I will take care of the farm, and your life is just the same, understand?"

Mark ate his last forkful, resenting her words. She made it sound as if the farm weren't his home, too.

"Good. Now clear these dishes and then hit that math book." She stood up, briskly, trying to act like her normal self, so Mark did the same. But she was wrong. The farm had everything to do with Mark. First they were going to turn it into a crazy-quilt farm, which everyone in 4-H was going to laugh at, like they laughed at the Fogelmans. And then he wasn't going to be part of 4-H anyway, because they weren't going to buy him a calf.

Mark waited until he was getting ready for bed, which was often a good time to talk to his mother, before he raised the calf issue with her. "Don't you think I should have a calf? Bobby and Jerry always get their own."

"Yes, Mark, there should be calf money for you. Of course, then there's feed. You might have to get a job when school's out, to help pay for the feed." She looked absently at the wall. "I'm not sure what you could do. Maybe Mr. Fogelman could give you something."

"But Mom, Bobby said they're going to Rochester this weekend. That's in two days. So could you get the money for me tomorrow?"

"Tomorrow? Well, hold on, what's the rush? I've got some bookkeeping to do first. We need to know just where we are, Mark. Where would you be thinking of keeping this calf, anyway? You're not thinking of fencing pasture, are you? You know we can't spare the land, and the fencing material, even barbed wire, costs—"

"But Mom, they're going to Rochester on Saturday. All of them. It's my chance. And Uncle Robert can help me pick a good one. Mom, all the boys are raising calves this year."

"Well, Mark, I think I better talk this over with your father."

"Tonight?"

"No, not tonight. Later. Mark!" She rattled his bed-sheet impatiently, as if he were a troublesome puppy that she was trying to put out the door. "Now get into bed, I've got to give Jessica a kiss. Did you brush your teeth?"

"No," he lied, and stomped off to the bathroom, where he ran the water and made angry faces in the mirror. No trip to Rochester. No calf money. He swore to himself not to go back to 4-H. Ever. He'd quit. He'd quit, and then Thelma would get all concerned and call up his parents and ask them what was wrong, and they would have to admit that they wouldn't even give him money for a calf.

When he got back to his room his mother was gone, so he got out his coffee can full of money. He had saved up allowances and presents from Grandma and money from a few odd jobs he had had.

He counted out twenty-five dollars and nineteen cents. No help there. He put it back and got into bed, angry. "And just remember, Mark, this has nothing to do with you," he whispered to the dark, in angry imitation of his mother.

On Friday he avoided Bobby and Jerry in school, except to mention casually that he couldn't go to Rochester on Saturday. "Got to help my dad," he muttered.

He felt a little better after he had explained his problems to his friend Paul Johanssen, but not much.

Paul was all set to get a hog in another week.

"I guess I could take one of my dad's hogs," Mark admitted, as much to himself as to Paul.

"Your dad has good hogs," said Paul. "And he knows all about them, he could help you."

"I know."

"You and I could end up showing together at the fair."

"I know."

"You'd probably do better than me, because your dad knows so much about hogs. My dad doesn't know anything, he just sells farm equipment."

"Your dad has a good job."

"Well, not so good," Paul admitted. "Too many farm families leaving, not so much business."

"Yeah, I guess so." But still, Paul got money for 4-H. Mark turned away jealously, just wishing the day would be over.

But on the bus, when he was ready to relax and see whether the fields were drying, here came Emma, holding Lisa by the hand, heading straight for him. Mark looked out the window.

"Lisa, you sit back with Jessica. I'm going to sit with Mark."

"No, I wanna sit with you." Mark smiled encouragement at Lisa. She was very small, so small she used her hands to get onto the seat of the bus. Everything about her was small, her nose and her hair and especially her fingernails.

"No, you sit there. You can still see me. Hey, Mark, how come you didn't come to 4-H?"

"Because I didn't feel like it."

"You should have come. Thelma's moving away. All of a sudden."

Mark sat up and moved his books aside to make room for her. "How come?"

"They said her husband had an accident with the anhydrous, he got real sick. And she kind of freaked out. But we had a new 4-H leader. Guess who? He used to live on our road." She giggled.

Mark groaned. "You're kidding! You mean Mr. Fogelman?"

"Yup. Not the old one, the young one who moved out and got his own farm. I hear it's even wilder than his father's. He raises goats, and he sells the milk for goat cheese. And he wants to make a wild duck sanctuary on the farm."

"Oh, gosh. I'm finished. I'm never going back to 4-H. Listen, Emma, I might as well tell you. Our farm is in trouble. I don't know why, it isn't fair, but the bank made trouble for my parents, and now they won't even give me money for a calf. So I can't even do a 4-H project. Unless I do a hog, but I won't."

Lisa turned around just then and gave him a glorious

24

smile. "We're going to Cob Town," she said.

"Good for you," grumbled Mark.

"We're going to the sale barn."

"Who wants to go to that stupid little auction, anyway?" Mark felt bad, being mean to a little kid, but he couldn't help it. "They don't sell anything, anyway."

"The new 4-H guy didn't talk about calves or pigs," Emma went on.

"What'd he talk about?"

"Money."

The school bus crossed the river, which had settled down now into a normal flow, still brown but not as dark as before. It was brown with dirt, the kind that ran out of the cornfield when it rained. The alders along the banks had tiny green leaves that looked like pale green haze as the bus whizzed past.

"What about money?" asked Mark.

"I have some money," said Lisa. "I'm going to buy something at the auction."

She was dumb, but she was cute. "What are you going to buy?" asked Mark.

"I'm going to buy . . . um . . . a llama."

Mark laughed. "Good for you. And while you're there, pick up a camel for me, would you? How much do camels cost?"

"Um . . . two dollars."

"He wants us to keep an account of our projects, in

25

a notebook," said Emma, going back to 4-H. "He said we should try to buy cheap animals, not expensive ones. He said he's going to give a prize for the most profit, not for the best animal, like the fair gives."

"What kind of a prize?"

"A hundred dollars."

The brakes squealed and the door whooshed open. "Hey, Halvorsens!" Mitch called. Emma jumped up quickly, gathering her book bag and Lisa's hand, and left. But she called over her shoulder, "You want to come to the Cob Town sale barn with us tomorrow?"

And Mark heard himself answer, "Okay."

The little sale barn in Cob Town was selling hogs first. Mr. Halvorsen was only interested in the calves, so after he had registered as a bidder, he took the four children into the little lunchroom for a snack. Jessica was pretending to be a reporter, with a spiral notebook and a pencil. Mr. Halvorsen had a cup of black coffee and a doughnut, and the children each got a huge piece of rhubarb pie. There were only a couple of other farmers in there, complaining about how wet it was and how they couldn't get their tractors into their fields for planting. When the pie was finished, Mark and Emma decided to go watch the animal sale. Emma remembered to tell the waitress how good the pie was.

Outside, they watched a long livestock trailer pulling

up to the chute, letting animals out into the pens behind the barn. This load was about thirty sheep, including some lambs. One little lamb looked only a few
days old and almost got lost in the crush as the farmer
shooed the animals out of the trailer. Then the mother
sheep got nervous and began to bleat, until the man
picked the lamb up and set it beside her.

"Do you like the little lambs, Lisa?" asked Emma,
who was again holding her sister by the hand.

"No, I wanna go in back," said Lisa stubbornly.

"All right. Come on."

The children followed the passageways through the
barn that led to the pens. Several farmers were back
there, looking over the animals they might want to
buy, while in the background you could hear the high
droning voice of the auctioneer as he reeled off numbers faster than Mark could think.

"Here's a little calf, Lisa," Mark tried.

"No, no, lookit over here. Chickens!"

There was a great mess of them, clucking despon-
dently, penned in three separate wooden crates with
slats on the sides. They were dark red in color, with
short, sharp beaks, and they all seemed to be hens,
though Mark realized he knew next to nothing about
chickens.

"Those are cute," said Emma, without much enthu-
siasm.

27

"They're ugly," Mark assured her.

"Do they lay eggs?" Lisa asked.

"I suppose so," answered Emma.

"Do they go cock-a-doodle-do?"

Mark laughed. "No, Lisa, not these chickens."

"Do you eat them?"

"If you want to," Mark answered.

"Hey, Mark, you could raise chickens," suggested Jessica. "For 4-H."

"What would I want to do that for?" Mark had brought his money along. In some hopeless way, he thought there might still be a calf, some very young or perhaps even injured or sick calf, that would be selling for about thirty dollars. And he might be able to nurse it back to health, and have a project after all.

"Eric says we should try different animals," said Emma.

"Who's Eric?"

"Mr. Fogelman. The one who talks about money. Maybe chickens don't cost very much."

"Buy the chickens, Mark," said Lisa solemnly. She took hold of his hand, looking up at him.

"So what if they don't cost very much?" Mark laughed. "What would I do with them?"

"Sell the eggs," said Emma.

"Right. And what does this guy say about flowers, Emma? He like that idea?"

"He said flowers might be okay. Very low input, that's what he said. And you can sell them. Did you ever notice there's a guy sometimes near the super-market, selling flowers out of his truck?"

"You mean trying to sell flowers. I never saw anyone buy some." Still, she was right, there really was a man who sold flowers, although Mark had never thought about him before. He must have a greenhouse, or maybe he drove up from the south.

Lisa was tugging Emma back into the main part of the sale barn. They saw Mr. Halvorsen sitting on the bleachers with his ticket in his hand, marking down what he bought. They were selling cattle now. The animals were chased in one door, sometimes one at a time, sometimes several in a lot to be sold together. A computer screen beside the auctioneer showed the weight of the animals, and the buyers bid at a certain price per pound. Jessica began writing the prices in her notebook.

Mark watched carefully. A few calves were going for as low as eighty cents a pound, but some of them looked sick, or had lame legs or open sores. You never could tell whether an animal like that would get well, and medicine might be expensive. The best calves were going for a dollar a pound, or even more, and none of them weighed less than three hundred fifty pounds.

Half a dozen other men were bidding along with

Mr. Halvorsen. They all seemed to know exactly what they were doing. Talking numbers without a break, the auctioneer would look from one to another, and each would immediately give a sign. Each one had his own style; one man nodded or shook his head, Mr. Halvorsen waved his index finger, and one man's sign was so small Mark couldn't tell what it was. Maybe he blinked. But the auctioneer seemed to know. "Sold!" came the call, and the door slid open at the other end of the enclosure for the cow to exit.

At last the doors opened to let an animal in, and nothing came. The auctioneer craned his neck around to see what was happening.

"That's all the cattle," called one of the helpers. "We've got this miscellaneous item." Two men carried in the chickens, and set the crates on the floor in front of the auctioneer.

The waiting men laughed a little.

"Where's this lot from?" asked the auctioneer, in surprise. "We don't handle chickens."

"We do today," answered the helper. He handed a paper to the auctioneer.

"All right," said the auctioneer with a smile, reading the paper. "We have here fifty Rhode Island Red laying hens, just coming of laying age. Owner died. They leave a minimum bid on this lot, Bob?"

The helper shook his head. "No information."

The auctioneer shrugged. "All right folks, who'll give me ahundredIsaidahundreddollarsforfiftychickens- that'sonlytwodollarsahenyoucanhaveayearofSunday- dinnersahundredahundredI'lltakeseventyfive—"

Lisa looked up at Mark. Jessica grinned at him; Emma looked at him hopefully. He could feel his heart begin to pound. If he really tried, he could hear the numbers racing by. They were coming down. Nobody wanted chickens.

"FiftydollarIsaidfiftydollar—now folks, these are nice fat hens, anyone wants to go into the egg business, here's your chance—fiftyfiftywho'llgivemeforty. . . ."

A man laughed when the auctioneer said "egg busi- ness," and most of the people were smiling.

"Why don't they bid?" Mark asked Mr. Halvorsen quickly.

He shrugged. "Nobody around here does chickens. Most of these guys are professional buyers for the pack- ing houses. Nobody has a chicken house. You know. It's just not what they came for."

The auctioneer was down to thirty dollars. Mark gripped the money in his pocket, afraid of what he was about to do. The auctioneer's voice went careen- ing on.

"TwentyseventwentyseventwentysixIsaidtwenty- fivewho'llgivemetwentyfive—"

Mark shot his hand up in the air.

"Sold!" yelled the auctioneer, before Mark could draw breath.

Mark lowered his hand. All around, people were smiling and looking at him, chuckling a little. What had he done?

Emma nudged him. "You should have waited. You might have got them for less."

Mark realized that this was true. He looked up at Mr. Halvorsen, but he was nodding his approval. "Good investment, son. You got an excellent price. We'll just load up my new calves, then, and heave the chickens in after them. I guess you've got tomorrow pretty well filled, then."

Mark looked blank. Tomorrow?

"You've got to build a chicken house tomorrow," he explained with a chuckle.

"It'll make a great news item," said Jessica seriously.

Mark took a deep breath. Lord, what if it did get into the paper? MARK SWENSON RAISES CHICKENS BECAUSE HE CAN'T AFFORD A CALF. What did a chicken house look like? Where would he get the materials? He had spent all his money on the chickens.

32

3

....

The chickens spent Saturday night in the little room in the barn where spare machine parts were kept, what Mark called the "nuts and bolts room." It was the only space he could think of that would contain them.

"You better give them some water," his father reminded him. "And I'm afraid you'll have to clean up the mess thay make in there."

They did make a mess, too—in one night they spread an amazing amount of droppings around, along with some feathers. They had spilled the water, too, and they clucked in what Mark could only think was an expectant way. He gave them some hog feed for breakfast, until he could figure out what he was supposed to feed them.

But as Mark turned to go and get some breakfast for himself, one of the hens set up a squawking and singing, her raucous voice going up and down over and over, *ka ka kawaaaakaka.* She was turning around and around at the same time, and then she flapped her wings, as if calling for everybody's attention. She had been sitting quietly over in a corner on top of some old packing shreds that had been left in their cardboard box. Now she came right out into the middle, squawking and flapping.

And there in the box, in a soft dent in the packing stuff, lay a brown egg. Mark put his hand on it. It was warm and smooth, and it fit perfectly into his hand, being just a little small for an egg.

Mark walked to the kitchen and held it out to his mother.

"Oh, my word," she said. "They really are chickens!"

Mr. Swenson laughed. "Did ya think we can't tell a hen from a rooster, Addy?" He took a cup of coffee from the pot and sat down at the table. "Well, make us some scrambled eggs, why don't you?"

Now she laughed. "It would take half a dozen of these to feed you two. Besides, I can't cook that, it's still warm. What if it has a baby chick in it?"

"It won't," her husband promised. "You hear any

rooster crowing this morning? No? Then there's no baby chick in that egg, guaranteed. I know that much."

"Then I'll fry it for Mark," she said. "Jessica's not up yet. Mark, you're going to be proud of these chickens yet."

"That hen is proud enough already; she doesn't need any encouragement. Dad, can I use that little shed, that used to be a pump house? For the chickens?"

"I knew you were going to ask that." Mr. Swenson took a sip of coffee, then set his cup down slowly, wiping his mouth. "What can you pay me for this shed, supposing I let you use it?"

"Hey, come on, Dad. You're not using it for anything."

"Supposing I decide to raise a pair of ostriches this spring?"

Mark glanced up, but his father was smiling. "You getting ready to plant today, Dad?"

His father sipped at the coffee again. "Too wet to plant. I already took the Deere out and got stuck once this morning. I'm headed over to Fogelman's again."

"To see how he plants?"

"And what he plants, and when, and all the rest of it. He's got this system called ridge-till planting."

"You sure he doesn't use any chemicals? Any at all?" Addy asked.

"No, I don't think he's that rigid about it. He uses

herbicide once in a while. But he's got some real low per-acre input. That buckwheat, now, does real well. Inexpensive to plant, and he sells directly to the Japanese."

"He know you're coming?" she continued, placing a very small egg in front of Mark, along with a couple of hefty pieces of toast.

"Yes, he does, as a matter of fact. You know, Addy, we never passed much time with those folks, but he's a very friendly guy."

"What's a per-acre input?" asked Mark.

"It's how much you spend on an acre," answered his mother. "For seed, chemicals, fuel, whatever it takes."

"You don't need to spend much to have acres that look all ratty like his," Mark scoffed.

"Mark!" scolded his mother.

"Well, Mom, you should—oh, Mom, this egg!"

"What's the matter with it?"

"Oh, Mom, you gotta taste it. Dad, Dad, try this. I never knew an egg could taste like that! I thought eggs were just, you know, Mom, here—" Mark thrust a forkful of egg at his mother, who slid it into her mouth obligingly.

"Very good," she said, swallowing. "Yes, Mark, I'd say that's very good."

"Let me see that," said Mr. Swenson, grabbing his

own fork and taking a piece. Mark watched his face carefully. He put his fork down. "Well, I thought maybe from what you said it was gonna taste like chocolate cheesecake. What it tastes like is an egg. But, yes, Mark, it's a very good egg. Must be because it's so fresh, what do you say? You notice the way that yolk stood up high in the air?"

"Dad, when you get back from the Fogelmans', can you help me with a chicken house?"

"Well, I might. Hello there, pumpkin." Jessica was coming barefoot into the kitchen, her brown hair rumpled.

"How come I didn't get an egg?" She sat at her empty place, staring at Mark's plate.

"Because you're a lazybones and you didn't get up in time," Mark explained.

"The early bird catches the egg, I guess." Addy brought Jessica a bowl of cereal. "Eat up, honey. This afternoon we'll all help Mark with his chicken house."

"Can I write about the chickens for the paper?"

"She isn't going to publish your dumb old stories in the real newspaper, are you, Mom?"

"We publish anything really newsworthy. Now run along and don't be rude to your sister. I've got some ads to write before I can help you."

Mark went out to inspect the pump house by himself. It was big enough, but the chickens would be healthier if they had a yard to scratch around in. They would also need nesting boxes and a roost to sleep on; he and his father had looked up chickens in one of his father's books last night.

Then there was the question of location. The pump house was not in a good spot, but maybe his father could move it. Mark picked out a place down near the river and not far from the Halvorsens' land. It would be out of the way of the big machinery, it would be off to the side of the field, and Mark could take water directly from the river. And the south slope there would be good, because chickens like plenty of light. They would also get some afternoon shade from the trees near the river; the book said that chickens don't like to get too hot.

The first step, which Mark could do himself, was to make nesting boxes. He rummaged for spare lumber in the barn, then measured carefully. He checked the book again for the correct size, and asked his mother for permission to use the electric Skilsaw.

"All right, but be careful."

"I will."

He drew lines where he needed to cut and held the boards firmly with his foot, as his father had taught him. Don't cut through the cord, he remembered. Squeeze the trigger slowly. Start the saw before you bring it to the wood.

Vroom! The loud noise still made him jump. The saw vibrated in his hand. He brought the blade carefully to the line, hearing the high whine as the teeth bit into the wood. *Clonk!* The cut piece fell to the floor, and he released the trigger. That was one.

Happily, Mark continued his work, cutting and nailing, measuring, thinking, until he had eight nesting boxes. He nailed them in place along the wall of the pump house. With a hand saw, he cut a little door for the chickens to go in and out, and then he put the block of wood back in place with hinges, so the door could be closed at night to keep out raccoons or foxes.

It was late Sunday afternoon before the chicken house was ready to move. Mr. Swenson explained how they could jack the whole house up onto a couple of two-by-fours, and then they could attach it to a tractor and pull it wherever they wanted. Whenever the chickens scratched up their yard too badly, they could move the house a few feet. Mr. Swenson said Mark could drive the tractor while he directed. Mark was not allowed to drive the big Deere, the one that had stuck in the mud yesterday morning, much less the huge Steiger, which was worth a hundred thousand dollars if you bought one new. Mr. Swenson had bought it used, two years ago. Its tires were taller than he was, and it had an air-conditioned cab with a tape deck and a computer with flashing lights.

The tractor Mark drove was a Farmall. It was over forty years old, but it still ran fine. Its tires were less than half the size of the Steiger's, and it had no cab at all, just a metal seat open to the air. It was good for odd jobs, and anyway, Mr. Swenson said, it was actually less likely to get stuck, being lighter.

Mark started the Farmall's engine and backed it out of the machine shed. Shifting gears carefully, he drove around to the pump house, where his father was holding the big chain with a hook to attach to the tractor. Mark had to back up just right, straight in line with the pump house, close enough so his father could attach the chain, but not, of course, close enough to hit him. Mr. Swenson helped by signaling to him when to cut the wheels, when to stop.

Now it was time to cross the barnyard and start down the hill. Mark put the tractor in low gear and started slowly. The chicken house lifted slightly, creaking. Mark stopped.

"You're okay!" his father yelled over the rattle of the old engine. "Just go slow."

Mark started again. He whipped his head forward and back, watching where he was going and what was happening to the chicken house. He had to drive around the planter, waiting in the yard, with enough space to spare so the chicken house would not hit it. He saw his dad give him the "perfect" sign.

Then he picked up to about ten miles per hour. The house rode nicely down the smooth slope until Mark made a slow turn to leave it on the level place that they had picked out. Relieved, he turned off the engine and waited for Mr. Swenson to unhook him.

"Great job, Mark. You drive that thing like a pro. I guess we'll have to have you up on the Deere this spring."

Mark tried to hide his pleasure, without knowing why. "Can we move the chickens in now?" he asked.

"Let's wait till tomorrow. I'll get wire for a yard tomorrow," he promised. "I've got to go to Rochester anyway, for buckwheat seed. Tonight we'll study up what kind of feed we should get."

"But I spent all my money."

"That's all right. We'll put it on the bill, and you can pay me back as you sell eggs. Your feed will just be, you know, mortgaged."

Mark smiled. "I get it now."

They rode the tractor together back to the house, where Mrs. Swenson was sitting at the computer.

"How's it look?" her husband asked her.

She turned around, making a sour face. "There's a note here from the federal insurance. If we don't plant by the middle of next month, we lose the crop insurance."

Mr. Swenson nodded and started a fresh pot of coffee. "Clouds moving in again" was all he said.

Mark's happiness about the chicken house faded. There was darkness behind the bright yellow curtain that framed the window behind the kitchen sink. Clouds from the west. How they had hoped and prayed for them in drought years.

"That's blowing over toward Cob Town," said Addy. "That one'll miss us."

Charlie Swenson shrugged and smiled at his son. "That mother of yours, she knows the most amazing things about the weather. We ever get poor, we'll just put her on TV and make a million."

"I'll have to get my hair done," Addy mocked him. But she was right about the rain, this time—the storm blew past with hardly a trace of water, and in the morning, when Mark got up for school, he learned that his father had already been out planting for two hours.

"Will Dad come in for breakfast?"

"I doubt it. I'll take him something on my way to the paper."

"I thought he had to go to Rochester for seed."

"I'll go myself this afternoon. If I'm not back, you're in charge of Jessica. Make her a snack."

"Don't forget the wire and the chicken feed. Did Dad tell you?"

"He told me. I won't forget."

Jessica looked up from her cereal. "Since Mark has chickens, can I have a rabbit?"

"Not this week. Did you brush your hair and teeth this morning?"

"Are you going to publish my auction story in the paper?"

"Not this time. You keep trying, though. Of course, it has to be something that Cindy likes an awful lot." Cindy was the chief editor and publisher of the Cob Town paper.

Mark grabbed his books, dodged his mother's kiss, and headed for the bus.

"Wait for me!" Jessica jumped up with a wail.

"Hurry up then, slowpoke."

Emma got on the bus with a seed catalog. She sat beside Lisa, showing her the pictures, but Mark was sitting right behind so he could look over the seat.

"You still planning to plant flowers and sell them?" Mark asked.

"Well, Grandma says it's a good idea not to put all your eggs in one basket."

Mark groaned. "Chicken jokes."

"Oh!" Emma clapped her hand over her mouth and laughed. "Mark, I didn't mean it. I just meant, you know, maybe I should plant several things. That way, if one thing doesn't sell or doesn't grow, there's always something else."

"Grow something people like a lot," Mark suggested.

"I already started tomatoes in little boxes."

Slowly, Emma turned the pages of the catalog. There were plenty of things to like: carrots, broccoli, cabbages, peas, spinach, or watermelons. Or how about pumpkins, for fall carving? No eggplant or squash, they agreed on that, anyway.

"Strawberries," said Lisa at last.

"Strawberries! That's it!" exclaimed Emma.

"But they don't grow from seed," Mark reminded her. "You have to buy strawberry plants. It costs more."

"Ouch. You're right."

"What's arugula?" asked Mark, looking at the gourmet page.

"Yuck. Looks like lettuce. Okay, here's what I think," said Emma. "Cornflowers, because if you don't sell them fresh you can dry them and sell them all winter."

"That sounds good."

"And carrots. Because everybody likes them."

"Okay. But they're not too exciting."

"And green beans," she went on, paying no attention. "And watermelon, because they'll be ripe later. See, it says ninety-two days. That's how long it takes to get ripe ones."

44

"And radishes," suggested Mark. "See, twenty-two days. That way you'll have something to sell real soon. And we can go around to people together—you can sell vegetables and flowers, and I can sell eggs."

Emma thought it was a great idea. "I'm going to make a diagram of the whole thing," she said. "And bring it to Mr. Fogelman. I mean Eric."

All day Mark looked forward to letting his chickens out in their yard, but when he got home his mother was still not back with the wire. He made Jessica some peanut butter and celery, gave Oscar a dog biscuit, filled the hog feeders, and fed the chickens some table scraps, which they seemed to like. He didn't hear the pickup in the driveway until after six. Running out to see, he found his mother in her frazzled mood. "Yes, I remembered the wire. We've got to keep a list right on the refrigerator, Mark, of what you owe us. I got fifty pounds of feed, and that was six seventy-two. If you mix it with corn it'll still only last a couple of weeks. Have you put potatoes on for supper? Have you done your homework? Hurry along, now. Jessica, get your papers off the table, get those tomatoes out of the fridge and wash them. How come no one has fed Oscar?"

Charlie Swenson was late for supper, but he was happy. He washed his hands and face at the kitchen sink, still in his field clothes coated with soil.

"Aren't you going to change before you eat?" Addy asked him.

"Just going out again after. Long as it's dry, I'll keep planting. Besides, this is only dirt."

"I know," she said with a smile. "The washing machine is getting a real rest. It's a relief, in a way, not to have all the chemicals around."

When Charlie was handling herbicides or pesticides, he never came into the kitchen in his field clothes. He would change completely, and the clothes would be washed all by themselves each time, and then the washer would be run with nothing in it, just to clean it out. The chemicals were that bad. But now Charlie sat down at the family table, dust and all. "I planted a hundred sixty acres so far," he said.

The whole family smiled.

On Tuesday afternoon the school bus passed the Deere working at the far end of another field. It was odd to see the planter working on a field that was still green, but Charlie had this new idea from Mr. Fogelman. He was leaving most of the weeds in place, just scraping off a narrow row where the seed went in.

"Is that Dad?" asked Jessica, who couldn't tell one tractor from another, and even forgot which fields they owned.

"Sure is. Look at him go. Man, he must be ripping

along." Mark felt hopeful, in spite of himself. Maybe the corn would outgrow the weeds. Maybe his father could save enough on chemicals to make the mortgage payments. Just like the chickens—maybe they would lay enough eggs to pay for what he owed on feed.

His mother was at home in the kitchen this day, and the kitchen table was strewn with little paper blocks and triangles. There was no room to make a snack.

"Hey, Mom, what are you doing?" asked Jessica, tossing down her math book so the wind made several pieces of paper skate around.

"Hey, stop that. I'm celebrating the planting. And the paper has gone to the printers, so we can forget about that for a day or two. I'm planning a quilt. What do you think?"

Mark looked at the bits of paper as his mother rearranged them. They could form star shapes or spirals or stair steps. He pushed some around himself. "What color will it be?"

"I'm not sure. Jessica, why don't you get us your crayons, and we'll experiment."

The CB crackled, and Addy picked it up. Mark could tell it was his father's voice, mad, but he couldn't make out the words.

Addy's expression changed. "You want *me* to?" she asked twice.

Finally she put the speaker down, turning to Mark,

sweeping the little paper pieces away with one hand. "Mark, he's stuck in the field again. He can't get out. He's got to keep moving. Come on, we're taking the Steiger to go pull him out. Jessica, you stay here."

"But, Mom, you don't know how to drive it."

"Neither do you." He could see she was determined, so he jumped up from the table to follow her out the kitchen door and across the yard to the Steiger. She got in first, raising her leg unnaturally high for the first step of the ladder into the cab, reaching up for the handholds. She was almost an inch shorter than Mark, and Mark could barely make it.

They sat side by side on the bench seat in front of the controls. "You've watched Dad do it," Addy said. "Now watch me, and if I do anything different, let me know."

"Okay." Mark saw his mother's fingers tremble slightly as she reached for the key, but she turned it firmly and the engine started. She ran quickly through all the gears, whispering their names: low, two, three, forward, reverse, high for the highway. She pointed to a lever. "What's that?"

Mark thought. "I think it's the hydraulic lift. You know, for the planter. But there's nothing connected there now."

"Okay." Smiling a little, Addy started the huge tractor forward, straight out to the road. Sitting way up high like this, they could see that no cars were coming for nearly a mile in either direction, so she did not stop, but turned directly into the road and shifted into high gear. The giant machine went bowling along nicely now at thirty miles per hour, though it seemed to take up the whole road. Mark and his mother grinned at each other.

"Want to turn on a tape?" asked Mark.

His mother rolled her eyes. "Don't touch a thing, Mark Swenson."

The field was over a mile away, but as soon as they came over the little rise in the road they could see the Deere, not moving, in a low spot in the huge green field. Addy slowed as she turned onto the grassy farm road that ran alongside the field.

"He could come take it from me now," she muttered.

"Why should he? You're doing great."

"I am, aren't I?" They grinned at each other again as Addy headed straight across the dirt of the field, toward the Deere. They could see Charlie now, leaning against a tire, but still somehow expressing frustration with his whole body. He didn't say a word when Addy finally stopped and opened the cab door, he just grabbed at the noisy chains that he held ready in his hand.

"Back her up another foot!" he yelled.

Addy eased the tractor backward a fraction.

"Stop, stop! What's the matter with ya?"

Addy rolled her eyes at Mark again. They both knew he was not really mad at them.

"Forward! All right, hold it right there. Now when I get in the Deere, I'm going to signal you when to move. Don't move until I signal. You got that?"

She nodded. Mr. Swenson got in the Deere, fiddled with gears, signaled. In the lowest low, Addy pressed the gas pedal. The Steiger lurched. The chain snapped tight. The wheels began to slip, churning up mud. Mark turned back to look and saw his father signing furiously.

"He says cut it, Mom."

The wheels stopped. Mr. Swenson climbed out again and adjusted the chains. Without speaking to them, he returned to the Deere. This time, at his signal, the Steiger began to move forward. Addy drove well; she kept the power going steadily and did not jerk or let the wheels slip. Inch by inch, the Deere followed them out of the low spot. The wheels hit drier ground.

"He says cut, Mom." Addy stopped again, smiling. This time they all climbed out of their vehicles, and Mr. Swenson was looking more relaxed as he unhooked the chain.

"Thank you, Addy. Sorry I yelled."

Mark's mother actually blushed.

"She's pretty good, for a town girl," he added, throwing a wink at Mark.

"Charlie," she growled. "Go plant your corn."

"You want to walk back, I'll bring the Steiger later," he said.

"We're driving." She heaved herself up the steps again. "Come on, Mark. Let's go see if Jessica's got that quilt figured out."

4

. . . .

By the time 4-H day rolled around again, it was May. The red maple blossoms near the river had turned to baby leaves, and you could smell the earth every time the sun peeked out, a heavy smell that followed Mark even into the classroom and made him think of mud and baby ducklings in the river and wild, dark, tornado skies. Mark had promised Emma he would come to 4-H.

Of course he asked Paul Johanssen about it first. Paul reported that Mr. Fogelman was nice, and only a little strange. "Don't you know him?"

"Sure, the old man's farm is on our road. Eric has

another farm, I'm not sure where. But he comes over sometimes."

Mark ran all the way from school to the church basement where they met, to get first dibs on the chairs. He wanted to sit in the back. But when he got to the 4-H room, he found that the chairs had been rearranged into a circle, so there was no back of the room to sit in. Mr. Fogelman was already there, and with one swift glance through his glasses he said, "Hello there, Mark Swenson. Where were you last time?" He was heavyset, like his father, and his red cap said International Harvester.

"I was . . ."

Eric sat down in one of the chairs in the circle. He moved calmly; Mark suddenly remembered how everyone at home these days seemed to be rushing around all the time, or else it was kids rushing out of the school bus, bells ringing, lining up, sitting down. Eric reminded Mark of a tree. He was listening.

"I was worried about my project," said Mark. That was not what he had intended to say. He had noticed that generally if you tell grown-ups you are worried about something, they tell you that you are not supposed to be worried about it—which leaves you with the same old problem, and the idea that you are an idiot as well.

"All good farmers worry, times like this," Eric observed carefully.

"My dad is worried. And my mom." Mark stopped and swallowed. His own worry was rising up in him, more than he wanted. Mr. Fogelman still listened. "They have money trouble. I don't know if I'm supposed to tell you. But everyone will know, anyway. They said they can't give me money to buy a calf, and raise it. I mean, last year Bobby Nelson—he's my cousin, you know?—he got a prize for his calf at the fair, and I want . . ." Mark took a long breath, so he wouldn't get a catch in his voice.

Eric waited for him, but Mark couldn't seem to say any more. "That must be a big disappointment," Eric suggested at last.

"Yes," said Mark simply. It seemed more manageable now. Like, okay, a disappointment.

"And so you have no livestock to raise for the fair?"

"Yes, he does!" Jerry and Bobby burst into the room together, with a gang of other kids close behind. Chairs scraped, book bags thumped onto the table, voices chattered, but Jerry's voice rang clear above all the hubbub. "He's got chickens!"

All the kids stopped to look at Mark, some of them laughing. Peter Miller began acting like a chicken, with his hands tucked under his armpits, squawking around in circles. Mark heard the words "laid an egg," and began to flush with anger. He noticed Emma coming in quietly, alone, setting her books carefully in a corner. He didn't want her to see all this.

Paying no attention to the noise, Mr. Fogelman nodded his head slowly at Mark. "Chickens." His deep voice sounded interested. Gradually the other kids got less noisy, and Jerry even turned to listen to what Eric was saying.

"Is that against the rules?" Jerry asked, sitting down in the next seat. "Can you really raise chickens?"

Eric raised his eyebrows and began to smile. "Rules? Are you speaking of the law that restricts agricultural output in the Midwest to swine and cattle, corn and beans? The one that was passed by, let's see, one Gerald Nelson, who had a perfectly good reason for it, let me see, I'll remember the reason in just a minute. . . ."

"Rules!" Now Bobby hooted at his younger brother.

"But this land is right for corn," Jerry whined. "And hogs, and cattle."

But Eric called the meeting to order. He announced that since most of the kids had already made an investment in an animal, this would be a good day to start the accounting system.

"Cool, accounting. That's what my brother's taking in high school," said a girl.

Eric showed them how to rule a paper the long way, and then he had them make headings of "Income" and "Expenses." "Anyone have any income yet?" he joked.

And then he added more seriously, "That's one of the problems. For farming, like most other businesses, you have to have some money before you can make money. That's because the income comes later. So for now, we'll pretend your parents are your bankers. You're going to borrow the money to get started, and then when you sell the animal or the product, you can pay them back."

"But not really, right?" asked Paul.

"Well, that's up to them. If it were me, I'd charge interest."

"I have to pay back," Mark announced. "My mom put the bill right on the refrigerator."

Bobby Nelson threw his pencil down on his paper. "Good thing I don't live at your place," he scoffed.

"Now, under outlays," Eric continued. "If you have already purchased an animal, write in the price." Most of the kids had written something already, Mark noticed. He saw Bobby write down $478, and he couldn't help whispering enviously, "Is he growing good, Bob?"

Bobby raised his thumb with a confident assertion. "But you should see Jerry's, he got the best. You coming over this weekend?"

Mark shrugged, covering his paper with his hand, where he had written $25.

"Now for the next entry, if you have already purchased some feed, put in the exact amount for that. If you borrowed feed from the family farm, put in what it's worth."

"How come?" asked a girl.

"Because we want to find out the true profit on your project. Or if it's actually costing your family money for you to raise this animal, we need to understand that."

"What if you don't know?"

"What if you can't remember?"

"We're going to keep careful records from now on," Eric promised. "I have a price list here, from the feed store, if anyone needs help. And I have a calculator, to help you multiply."

Paul was the first one to grab the calculator. Mark saw him multiply 12 bags of feed by $8.16, and heard him whistle under his breath when he saw the figure. "What does a hog sell for?" he asked out loud.

"Not enough," said a voice from the other end of the table.

But that was not all. When the first feed costs had been figured up, Eric wanted each 4-H-er to estimate the cost of boarding the animal. He said you had to go home and work it out with your parents. For instance, if you had a little pig in with twenty-four of your father's pigs, then you asked him what it cost to keep that part of his barn for the summer, and you had to figure up 1/25th of that. It didn't sound too bad until you started thinking about keeping a calf in a stall all to itself. Mark heard Bobby and Jerry muttering about letting their calves out to pasture, and then Eric was going on about the price of land, and fences, and interest payments.

"He's crazy," Paul muttered. "This is worse than math class."

"Just make your best estimates, and we'll look them over next time," Eric promised. And that was the end of the meeting. Not a word about animal nutrition, or keeping stock clean, or the best way to brush a cow, or the shots to give a young pig, or any of the things that Thelma Olson used to talk about. Emma was right—Mr. Fogelman was interested in money.

Emma's mother came to take them both home. "What did you put down for expenses?" Mark asked Emma, in the car.

"Twelve dollars for seed, so far." Emma looked quite pleased with herself. "And I'll have to pay my dad something for the tilling, about twenty bucks, I guess. Wow, that Bobby Nelson is going to have to get a lot for his beef, if he wants to beat me."

Mark decided he wasn't so badly off himself. He had paid way less than a tenth of what Bobby had paid for his animal, and Mark's only other expenses were feed and chicken wire. Chickens didn't eat as much as a growing steer. It was just barely possible that the chickens were going to turn out to be a good idea.

Rain came again. Mark heard it in the night, and early in the morning he heard doors slamming with the sound of his father's frustration. Even Emma was cross in school. She said it was time to set out her tomato plants, but the ground was too wet to till.

Sometimes the sun would shine for an hour, and then the clouds would gather again, covering the sky from horizon to horizon. The river ran high, and the farmers' pickup trucks were lined up outside the Eat Shop, where the grown-ups drank coffee and waited.

Every day after he finished the hog chores, Mark walked down to his chickens. He put fresh water in each of the watering jars, and he put laying mash in the feed troughs. He also sprinkled oystershell in the yard, for the chickens to eat as they pecked at the ground. Oystershell would give their eggs strong shells.

But at first there were no more eggs, though Mark looked carefully in the nesting boxes, and around the yard, too. His mother said maybe the hens were too young, or maybe they needed to get adjusted to their new home.

But one day there were two eggs; then there was one; then there were four. After the first dozen, Addy paid Mark for them, the same price she would pay in the store: seventy-nine cents. She didn't actually pay him the money. She started an account sheet. And she warned him that he'd better be on the lookout for more egg customers. Fifty chickens can lay three or four dozen eggs a day, once they get going.

On a Saturday near the end of May, Emma called to say that the ground had dried up enough for her father to rototill. Would Mark like to come and help her plant the garden?

There wasn't much happening at home—his father was off selling more of the pigs. So Mark agreed to help Emma. He rode his bicycle, but when he got to the Halvorsen house, Emma's mother directed him back toward his own place. Emma had located her garden near the Swensons', just up and over the slope above the chickens.

A big rectangle of dark earth was tilled up, and Mark knew by the sweetish smell that it was well treated with manure. Emma and Lisa were marking off spaces with strings tied to sticks. Emma stood up to wave hello.

"We have a map," Lisa announced, showing Mark a paper.

"It was hard to work out," Emma explained. "My grandmother helped me. Things have to be the right spaces apart, and you don't want the tall things to shade the short things."

Mark felt tired just looking at the plan. It included rows of corn and beans and carrots, thirty-six tomato plants, eight hills of watermelon, and of course the cornflowers. And way down at the end, two twenty-five-foot rows of radishes. If the garden grew, it was going to be a lot of food. "How are you going to weed all that?" he asked.

"My mom has this little power cultivator. She says I can rent it. That's why the rows are one foot apart, because the cultivator will just fit between them. She says if I do that every week, I shouldn't have much problem."

Mark went to work willingly enough on the tomato plants, where Emma had already marked the spaces. The work had a rhythm: dig a little hole, put in a handful of plant food, mix the soil in the bottom of the hole, place the plant gently, tamp down all around. On to the next plant.

"Where are you going to sell your vegetables?" Mark asked Emma.

"In town," she replied decidedly. "Right on the corner of Main and Hartland. You know where that empty lot is? Lisa has a big wagon, and we're going to put the best vegetables out in the wagon. Kind of a display."

Mark moved on to another plant, thinking. "And stand there all day?" he asked.

"We could sit." She stood up, wiping a fly from her

forehead, leaving a streak of dirt. "Not every day. Once a week. We could go always on the same day, so people would expect us."

Mark noticed that Lisa was looking at him hopefully, as if it were important that he approve of their plan. But he wasn't sure. "Sounds like a lemonade stand, like the comics," he said. "Maybe you should offer psychology, too. Like Lucy. 'The doctor is in.' "

Emma bent over her row of corn seed. "I was thinking of eggs," she said.

Mark brightened. "You would sell my eggs for me?"

"If you share the time with us."

"I'm helping you now," Mark pointed out. He was on his second row of tomatoes, and it seemed awfully long.

"We could feed the chickens, if you have to be away."

"I can feed the chickens," added Lisa.

Mark tried to picture the harvest: bunches of blue flowers, piles of sweet corn, bags of tomatoes. "We could be partners," he said more pleasantly. "We could have kind of like a co-op."

"I know," said Lisa. "Like Cob Town Co-op Grain Elevator."

"Lisa! Are you planting the radishes one at a time?" Emma came marching down the side of the garden to inspect, so Mark took a break to look over her shoulder.

"Oops, I forgot." Emma had made a straight furrow

across the garden, but Lisa had left little piles of seed here and there along it.

"I can fix it," Mark offered. He kneeled down beside Lisa, showing her how to hold the pile of seeds in the palm of her hand, letting one seed drop at a time as she moved along.

Emma got down beside him. "All right, then," she said. "Partners." She held out her earthy hand, and Mark shook it.

It was not at all like shaking hands with a grown-up. Grown-up hands were too big to get your fingers around, and then they always squeezed you too hard. Emma's hand was just the right size, and comfortable. Mark walked quickly back to the tomatoes with a funny feeling inside that made his face hot. But it was not a bad feeling, and he was glad that he was going to be partners with Emma.

5

·······

By the middle of June, when most of the corn had finally started to grow, the Swenson fields looked ratty, just the way Fogelman fields had always looked. Because Mr. Swenson had used no herbicide, the weeds had a great start between the rows, foxtail and morning glory, grasses and flowers. True, the corn seedlings were growing in the bare spaces that the planter had scraped between the weeds, but you couldn't tell that from the road, and Mark was embarrassed. It was like an advertisement to everyone that the Swensons couldn't farm. The Nelson fields looked right—dark black soil with razor-straight rows of bright green corn shoots.

Now that school was out, Mark went to help Emma with the garden nearly every day. The weeds grew and grew, but Mark and Emma kept after them, sometimes using the cultivator, sometimes pulling by hand. Lisa pulled up half the radishes by mistake, but it was all right, because there were too many anyway. Jessica helped once, but she stopped after a few minutes to count worms. When the afternoons got hot, they waded into the river, chasing water striders and slapping at mosquitoes.

On a Sunday evening Emma brought her grandmother over to inspect the garden and see the chickens. Mrs. Halvorsen walked slowly, with a cane, but you often saw her going about the farm. She seemed delighted with the chickens.

"That's the right way, to give them a yard," she said approvingly. "I don't like the modern way of raising chickens, all crowded into high-rises, no windows. These chickens will be happy. And you watch, they'll be healthier, too. We always kept chickens when I was a young woman." Moving deliberately, testing each step with her cane, she walked all around the chicken house, clucking like a hen herself. "What are you planning to do with the droppings?" she asked.

"Shovel them out the door, I guess," said Mark. He had already started a pile.

"Well, you save them for me."

"Grandma, can we put them on my garden?" asked Emma.

"Not this year. They need to compost down, or they'll burn your young plants. But you save it. I like the way you young people are working together. People don't always neighbor the way they used to. And Lisa can help, too."

"I can gather eggs," said Lisa proudly.

"Don't let Mrs. Chicken peck your fingers," warned her grandmother.

"Oh." Lisa put her hands behind her back.

Mrs. Swenson had come out, too. She greeted old Mrs. Halvorsen politely. "We don't see you about as much," she said.

"Oh, well, no, you see, it's harder now. And when it's rainy, my knees . . ." Mrs. Halvorsen brushed away an imaginary cobweb. "But I've heard you're doing a quilt. I'm so glad. You must let me come over and see the pattern."

"I don't get much chance to work on it. One thing and another."

"Oh, yes, I know how it goes."

Very soon the egg supply grew until it overflowed Mrs. Swenson's refrigerator, and then the egg rounds began. Mark was shy about finding customers, but Emma called nearly everyone she knew, and before long they had ten families to visit weekly, each with different orders for eggs and radishes. They would pick up the empty egg cartons at the same time, to reuse. One week Mark's mother would drive, the next week Emma's. And the children carefully noted the cost of the gasoline, under "Expenses."

The store price of eggs went up, so they raised their price, too. Now they were making ninety cents a dozen. In a good week, if they sold twenty dozen eggs, they made $18.00. They had already covered the cost of the chickens, plus half the feed. The balance sheet looked like this:

EXPENSES:	$25.00	purchase chickens
	28.00	chicken wire
	24.48	200 lbs. of laying mash
	10.00	100 lbs. of cracked corn
	3.83	50 lbs. of oystershell
	3.00	gas

TOTAL: $94.31

INCOME: Week #1			
May 7	3 doz. at $.70 =	$ 2.10
May 14	5 doz. at .75 =	3.75
May 21	8 doz. at .75 =	6.00
May 28	10 doz. at .80 =	8.00
June 5	16 doz. at .80 =	12.80
June 12	23 doz. at .90 =	20.70

TOTAL: $52.35

67

That left only $41.96 to make, and it would be pure profit from then on. Mark put his light back on at night, after his mother had turned it out, to stare at the figures. But he was so tired that after a few minutes they would swim in front of his eyes, and several times his mother scolded him when she found him fast asleep with the light on.

Bobby and Jerry stared at the figures, too. By the 4-H meeting on the 17th of June, Bobby was $437 in debt, and Jerry was worse, with $523. Beef was going for $1.10 a pound wholesale.

"Doesn't mean anything," Jerry pouted. "My big expenses are over with. The calf's going to weigh eight hundred pounds in August. You'll find out."

Mark looked over at Emma, who looked back, shaking her head skeptically.

On Friday of that week, when Mark got home, dirty and tired from the garden, his Uncle Robert was there, standing near the porch, talking to the Swensons. Jerry was with him.

"They tell me in town you didn't order anhydrous this year," Uncle Robert was saying. "You find a cheaper source, or what?"

"No, Robert, I didn't do anhydrous this year. None of those herbicides, either. No Atrazine. No fertilizer."

Uncle Robert adjusted his cap. "What are you doing for nitrogen, then?"

68

"Pig manure. I had a good supply."

"Poh!" Uncle Robert kicked the tire on his pickup and adjusted his cap again. "You're not going to rely on manure, are you?"

Mr. Swenson looked calm, but Addy answered nervously, "He's been talking to the Fogelmans. We've done soil tests, and we've got it all worked out. We think it's going to work, Bob. It's what we're going to try."

"Well, now, I didn't figure you were that bad off. You should come to me, Charlie." Uncle Robert spread his hand generously open. "I could help. God knows how, but family is family."

But now Mrs. Swenson shook her head more firmly, looking at her husband. "We've decided about it, Charles and I. It's what we want to do. We were interested in going that way before, you remember, but it was hard to take the risk of trying something new. Sometimes hard times push you a way you needed to go anyhow."

Uncle Robert looked dumbfounded. "You don't mean to say you're going organic?"

"Not strictly, no," said Mr. Swenson calmly. "I have no quarrel with chemicals, used sensibly, where you really need them. I'm going to try to make it without herbicide and pesticide this season, but could be I'll have to change my mind later."

"Why don't you change your mind sooner, and save yourself a lot of trouble! Listen, Charlie, you do what you want about fertilizer. I think it's madness, but I can't do anything about it now. But I'm ordering Atrazine myself, you hear?" Uncle Robert stood taller, but so did Mark's father. Mark could see the anger in both of them.

"You take care of your farm, and I'll take care of mine."

Uncle Robert backed away a step. "All right, all right. Forget it. It's all right." He adjusted his cap again, as if he were flipping the whole conversation away. "Let me see this blasted buckwheat you were boasting on."

Mark walked away, disturbed. At any rate, he had his chickens to tend, and then the regular hog chores still waited, though there were only a couple of dozen hogs left. He smelled pot roast from the kitchen, and his stomach growled.

Jerry tagged after him, to see the chickens.

"Those are them, huh," he said. "Man, they stink. I guess you're too poor to afford a calf, huh? My steer is gonna smear you."

Mark waded in among the hens, which swirled around his legs like running water. He didn't care what Jerry said. Jerry was just jealous because of the profits rolling in.

70

Mark poured the stale water out of each of the watering jugs and then carried them, two at a time, down to the river to fill. At least Jerry gave him a hand with that. Then Mark measured fresh feed into the troughs and cleaned out the floor area.

"Here's where the profit is," he remarked, taking his egg basket off its nail.

Jerry looked dubious. "So how many eggs you get in a day?"

"Watch." Mark moved carefully from nest to nest, feeling in the hay, enjoying Jerry's expression as he pulled two, three, sometimes even four or five eggs from each nest.

"Let me see," said Jerry. He went to the last nest in the row and plunged his hand in, coming out with two eggs in one hand.

"Careful," said Mark.

"And here's another." Jerry picked up a third in his other hand. "Here you go." He swung around quickly, but as he did so one of the eggs in the double hand dropped.

"Hey! See what you did? You wasted an egg. Now the hens are going to eat it. It's not good for them."

"Big deal. One egg." Jerry didn't look sorry at all. "Ha, look at them run. Why shouldn't it be good for them?"

"Because it teaches them to eat eggs. You don't know

anything about chickens. Get out, and let me clean this up."

"Okay, okay, take it easy. Here, I'll take the egg basket for you."

"You will not. You leave that basket right there, Jerry Nelson."

"All right, sorehead. Just because I broke one of your precious eggs. I'm going back to the house. Anyway, my dad says your dad is soft in the head these days."

"Get lost, you stupid jerk!" shouted Mark. Jerry ran away laughing.

Mark shooed the hens out of the way and picked up the bedding that still had egg clinging to it. He threw that onto the compost heap, and brought fresh. He bet to himself that Jerry had broken that egg on purpose, out of pure jealousy.

Mark took the egg basket straight to the barn and did his hog chores. Uncle Robert was still dawdling around the kitchen door, pulling nervously at his cap, and Mr. Swenson was standing squarely on both feet, not giving ground. Mark did not want to see them again. He did the chores slowly, feeling where his back and shoulder muscles were tired from the weeding. He didn't mind. He was making money now.

At last he heard the truck start up and drive off, but even then he dawdled, watching the pigs. The little ones came galloping up to the fence, pink noses wiggling. He hoped that his father was right, that the pig manure would be enough nitrogen for the cornfield. It was working on Emma's garden, right enough. So why not the cornfield? If only those weeds didn't choke everything out.

Mark went in only when his mother rang the bell for dinner.

The next morning, being Saturday, Mark sat late at breakfast. Jessica came down, shaking the hair out of her face. "I'm going to write a story about your co-op. You and Emma, and the 4-H contest."

"Oh, yeah? Mom going to put it in the paper?"

"I don't care. I'm going to interview Bobby."

"Oh." Mark sighed. Maybe he would ride his bike over to Emma's. Maybe he wouldn't; he was tired of hoeing. He kicked his chair leg for a while, and then ambled down to visit the chickens.

The henhouse was strangely quiet as he approached. No one laying an egg just now.

In fact, not a single hen was out in the yard. That was odd. It was a lovely morning.

Mark's surprise was so great that, when he looked in the door and saw an empty coop, his mind was blank. It was like a dream; it was something that couldn't be so. And then he thought, forty-two dollars, I still owe forty-two dollars, what am I going to do?

Only then did he realize the problem. The door was standing wide open. He hadn't opened it to look inside, it was just open. So naturally the hens had gone out. Where were they? Who had left the door open?

Standing there in the sunshine, half dazed, he heard a scream. He shook himself. Emma was almost flying over the rise, her hair, without any elastics, half blinding her, and she was screaming something at him.

"The chickens! Mark, the chickens!"

He started. "You found them? Where are they?"

"The chickens!" He noticed that she was trying not to cry.

"Are they all right? Hey, calm down. Tell me." She was close enough now to stop running and get a gulp of breath.

"The garden!" she screamed.

"What? The chickens are in the garden?"

She nodded, her face screwed and ugly. "Oh, Mark, they ate everything!"

Mark gasped. The chickens out, maybe half of them lost. Now the garden. "What do you mean? What are you talking about?"

"The chickens got into the garden. Either last night, or early this morning. Why can't you keep your darned chicken door closed? They pecked everything to bits. There aren't any more beans! No carrots!" Then she threw her hands in front of her face and just bawled.

Mark stared at her. And then he knew. Jerry Nelson! The rat!

6
■■■■■■

Emma was wrong. The whole garden was not destroyed.

Still, Mark felt a wave of despair. The chickens were pulling up carrot seedlings as fast as they could peck, and they had torn some of the bean plants to threads. A couple of hens were just starting in on the watermelon.

"All right," he said calmly. He felt like his father, talking about the bank calamity. "First thing we do, we're going to get the chickens back in the coop. Come on, we have to get some grain sacks out of the barn."

"You go," she said. "I'm going to try chasing them

out, because it will take you an hour to catch them all." She emphasized the *you*, as if it were all his fault.

There *was* sense in that, and anyway he liked Emma better angry than crying. "I'll get some corn," he said. "That way we can lure them out." He ran back to the barn, gathered an armload of the loose-woven burlap bags that the chicken feed had come in, and quickly poured several pounds of grain into one of the sacks. He was back at the garden, huffing, in ten minutes. Emma was running back and forth like some mechanical scarecrow, yelling "Shoo! Shoo! You ratty old bird. Shoo!"

"Here, chick, chick, chick," Mark called. He began to scatter the corn along the sides of the garden. A few chickens found it, and then a few more. Emma got behind the chickens and began shooing them toward the grain. As soon as most were out of the garden, Mark began grabbing them, one at a time, by the feet, and stuffing them into the grain sacks. Some of them squawked and sidestepped before he could get them, and a couple pecked him, but he kept at it.

After a few minutes of watching, Emma joined in. She wasn't as successful, because she hesitated before she grabbed.

"Here," said Mark, thrusting a bag of about ten chickens at her, "take these to the coop, and bring the bag back. And be sure to shut the door."

"Why don't you take your own advice once in a while, birdbrain," she shot back at him. Mark let her go; there would be time to explain later.

It took more than an hour to rescue all fifty chickens—or maybe it was about forty-seven or forty-eight, Mark had lost count. He no longer cared if a few were missing. Emma flopped onto the ground beside him, tucking carrot seedlings back into the ground as she sat.

"That won't work, you know," Mark advised her. "You can't transplant carrots."

"When I want your advice I'll ask for it."

"Listen, I didn't leave that door open."

"Then who did?"

"Jerry Nelson."

Emma stopped poking at the soil and looked up at him curiously. "How do you know that?"

Mark told the whole story, about how jealous Jerry was, how he had broken an egg on purpose, how he could easily have sneaked back to the coop after Mark left.

Emma just sucked in her cheeks and went back to fussing with the carrots. At last she said, "It's easy to drop an egg by accident. They're round and smooth."

"I never dropped one."

"Well, anyhow, you don't *know*."

But Mark figured he knew well enough.

By evening, the skies had clouded again and a light rain was falling. Shaking his head over his evening coffee, Mr. Swenson was disgusted. "Soil's soaked already," he said. "River's high. I can't bring that tractor within half a mile of the lower field. The corn is all planted, but it's past time for beans."

Addy was more philosophical about it. "Some seasons it rains, some seasons it doesn't. Hey, Mark, call up the weather man and order some sun, would you?"

"Supposed to clear by Monday," said Mark, who had been listening to weather reports, as his father wished.

"Attaboy. Well, Addy, looks like I could spend Sunday afternoon fixing the pump for the well. You got plans for Sunday?"

"I asked Robert and Sarah and the boys for supper."

"Oh." Mr. Swenson gave her a look.

"Don't think I don't know you had a tiff with Robert. But he's my brother. And they haven't been over since Robert's birthday. I expect good behavior." Arching her eyebrows at all three of them, as if they were naughty little children, she flounced out to the kitchen with the coffeepot. Mr. Swenson only chuckled, but Mark gave a big boo.

Mark wondered whether Bobby was in on the plot against the chickens, too. He was going to think of some way to get back at them, for sure, next time he went over there. He could take some of their darned Atrazine and stick it in the feed, so they couldn't use it. But he knew he wouldn't really do that.

It rained heavily all Saturday. Late in the afternoon, Charlie went to see if the river was rising. He came back with a shrug. "It's all right so far," he reported, "only risen maybe a couple of feet. It's holding the banks. If we're able to finish planting by next week, we'll be all right."

Just as Mark expected, Bobby and Jerry arrived looking perfectly innocent. It was Uncle Robert who seemed to have a chip on his shoulder, which Aunt Sarah was doing her best to cover over.

"Robert's had such a rough time this spring," she said, as he barely greeted Mr. Swenson. "Isn't the weather something awful? Addy, there's so much mud in the house, I think I'm going to scream half the time. There, boys, take your boots off on the porch, and don't mess your aunt's clean house." The rain was coming down heavier than ever.

Mark stood at the back of the kitchen, gazing at his cousins with what he hoped was a stony look.

"How are the chickens?" Bobby asked politely.

"Fine," said Mark, without a flicker. That shut them up nicely.

When everyone was comfortably settled around the table, the talk went better, until Uncle Robert remarked, "I see you have some weeds growing in your cornfields."

"Doesn't bother the corn," replied Mr. Swenson, chewing his potato.

"First time I ever heard that weeds don't compete with corn," Uncle Robert went on.

"Fogelman teach you that?" Bobby asked Mark, the scorn dripping from his mouth.

"At least we don't have half an inch of topsoil pouring into the river this spring, like a lot of farmers," Mr. Swenson answered for him, looking straight at his brother-in-law. "Fishing won't be worth a fly this summer. All the trout are going to be stuffed with anhydrous ammonia and topsoil."

"What are you talking about?" Uncle Robert put his fork down.

"Oh, fishing, Robert always did love to go fishing," chirped Aunt Sarah. "You know, he's always been so grateful, Charlie, for the fishing hole you showed him, where he got that big trout last year. Wasn't that just the funnest time?"

Everyone looked at her, trying to smile.

"We might plan the Fourth of July picnic for that spot," said Addy. "Only the way things are going this spring, I don't suppose the sun will come out for that, either. We may have to have the Fourth of July indoors."

"Fine with me," said Jerry, "long as we have fried chicken." He looked at Mark and smirked.

"I'm going to make more money than you are," Mark said angrily. "And I don't care what you try to do to me. You just watch out, because I know." He hadn't meant to say all that, but he was angry at them all for criticizing his father.

"What are you talking about?" asked Jerry.

"Mark!" That was his mother, and even his father was looking crossly at him. "Mind your manners."

"Well, why doesn't Jerry mind his own livestock, then?"

"What are you talking about?" asked Jerry again.

Mark couldn't stand the innocent sound of the questions. He jumped up, tipping his chair over backward, and he waved his fork, which unfortunately had a piece of potato on it that went flying into Aunt Sarah's hair.

"Mark!" That was his father now. "What's gotten into you, boy? You go upstairs to your room. Right now."

"But Dad, he—"

"Right now."

Mark shrugged and turned on his heel. He didn't want to stay, anyway; he'd be happy to get away from them all.

Upstairs, the rain was drumming on the roof harder than ever. Mark could tell by the rivery sounds that water was pouring broadside out of the gutters, because it was coming down faster than they could handle it. It was so dark outside that even when he turned out the light in his room, he couldn't see the tree outside the window.

He listened to the roaring, gurgling, watery sounds. Then above them, downstairs, he heard voices raised. They weren't paying any attention to the water; now Mark's father had gotten angry again, and was speaking loudly.

What if the river rose as high as the chicken house?

Mark ran softly down the stairs, grabbed his poncho from the hook in the hall, stepped out onto the porch, slipped his boots on, and ran toward the barn.

The lids of the hog feeders were quiet. The pigs were asleep. But the rain pelted madly against the silo, and the mud seemed to grab at his boots, slowing him down.

Beyond the barn, he listened. All he could hear was the rain coming down, and all he could see as he peered down the hill was empty blackness. He slowed, walking carefully now, using his ears.

Suddenly his foot stepped into water. He gasped. No, it was only a puddle. A few more steps, and then suddenly he saw, with his eyes newly adjusted to the dark. The river was rising, all right. He could see the outline of the chicken house, and just beyond it a blacker darkness that was the water. The water had left the trees and started up the slope; it was no longer river-shaped, but spread out like a lake, and here at the shallow edge it was not flowing fast, but it was creeping forward. And the first thing in its path was the chicken house.

He would have to get the tractor, drive it down here, and pull that old pump house to higher ground.

And he must hurry. He turned and ran back up the hill, with the mud like enemy hands now, pulling at his feet. He remembered how Bobby used to tease him, holding him by the ankles so he couldn't run away. He felt like that now.

He swung around the side of the equipment shed and flung open the door. Where were the keys? He hopped quickly into the seat and felt with his hand. Yes, they were just dangling there, in the ignition. He turned; the damp engine whined a moment in complaint, but then it turned over, and the tractor gave its reassuring chug-chug-chug.

Craning his neck around, he could just make out the edges of the shed, but he backed the tractor out smoothly and swung it around toward the river. The rain was slowing somewhat, and the wind was down. He heard the engine, and above that the wet sound of the large tractor tires turning confidently through the mud of the barnyard.

He came to the edge of the hill, and put the Farmall

into low gear to help slow it down. He could feel when the traction began to give, when the tires began to slip instead of turn. They had nothing to turn against; the farmyard had a thin layer of mud, but now the soil was deep and soft, and seemed to have turned to mush deeper and deeper.

"Come on," Mark said to the tractor. "Don't fail me now."

Suddenly the tractor was turning sharply without his willing it. He knew what was happening; one wheel was stuck while the other was still moving forward. He had to throw the lever that would put all the power into the stuck wheel. His hand groped for it in the dark, but he threw it the wrong way. The tractor spun right around until it was facing uphill, and it leaned over to one side so far that he had to hold on to the steering wheel to keep from falling out.

Mark swore. A tractor could fall over. He got the lever back where it should be. "All right, drat you," he said, "go uphill then."

But the tractor would not go uphill. He looked down; as he pressed the accelerator, ever so slowly, the big wheels were turning in place, digging themselves deeper and deeper into the muck. The mud was up to the hubs now. He was stuck, for sure.

Trembling with frustration, Mark turned off the engine and got down from the tractor. He ran down the hill; the rain had slowed to a drizzle, but the river was still rising fast, fed by the water running off the drenched fields for miles around. It would continue rising for hours after the rain stopped.

His boots stuck in the mud, but he pulled his feet out and left the boots behind. The mud was cold. And then he was in water up to his ankles. That meant that the floor of the chicken house was now under water. The chickens would still be dry, up on their roosts, but for how much longer?

Now he needed help. It was no good being proud, or trying to pretend that the Farmall wasn't stuck in the mud halfway down to the river.

He turned, and saw a light. Then he heard voices, exclaiming. They had come out to check on things at last, and they had discovered the tractor.

"Dad!"

"Mark! Is that you? What in blazes are you doing driving the tractor into a flood?"

"Dad! It's the chickens!" Mark had come up close to his father, who was holding a large electric lantern. Its beam lit up the pathetic sight of the tractor, mud-spattered and half sunk at an angle.

"Hey, Mark! What kind of an idiot are you turning into? You could have turned it over on yourself, you could have killed yourself."

"Charlie," objected Uncle Robert. He put his hand

out and drew Mark into the light. "Kid's been brave, Charlie," said Uncle Robert softly.

Mr. Swenson grunted, but he stopped berating Mark, giving him a chance to explain himself.

"The river's rising," Mark panted. "It's over the floor of the chicken house. We've got to move it to higher ground."

Bobby and Jerry were there, too, looking very clean, Mark thought. Bobby whistled. "Jeez, man, you were trying to move it yourself?"

Even Jessica was concerned. "How come you went all by yourself, Mark?"

Mark shrugged. "Everybody was fighting."

Uncle Robert laughed. "Well, that we were, and look who was tending to the farm. All right then, let's move a chicken house!" He gave a whoop and began leaping down the hill, mud splashing in great dollops behind him. With a look at each other, Bobby and Jerry followed, and then at last Mr. Swenson laughed, too. "Come on, Mark. All together, we can pull it out by hand."

Mr. Swenson was right. He and Uncle Robert took hold of the poles at opposite corners; Bobby took a third corner, and Jerry and Mark heaved on the fourth. Jessica stood behind her father, trying to help. At a signal from Uncle Robert, they all lifted, and the whole chicken house rose several inches off the ground. They staggered uphill a couple of feet and rested. They could hear the awakened chickens inside, muttering and clucking.

"Ready, set, heave!" They lifted and fought their way forward again.

"Careful! Don't run into that tractor," called out Mr. Swenson.

"Aim a little left on the next haul," called Bobby.

Three more lifts, and the chicken house was beyond the tractor, where Mr. Swenson judged it would be safe. "River's never come within six feet of here," he said. "And this flood'll be over by morning."

He pointed skyward, where the clouds were already blowing by, revealing a faint scrap of moon that peeked and hid and peeked out again.

Mrs. Swenson's voice called anxiously from the house, and they all yelled back.

"A hot drink would go good, though it is the end of June," suggested Mr. Swenson. They left the coop sitting at an angle in the mud, but Mark guessed the chickens wouldn't mind.

By the time Aunt Sarah and Mrs. Swenson were done fussing over them, cleaning some of the mud off them and serving coffee and hot chocolate, everyone seemed in a pretty good mood.

"Thanks for helping me with the chickens," Mark managed to say to his cousins.

"And me, too," put in Jessica. "I helped, too, didn't I, Mark?"

"Yeah. Thanks."

"Anyway," said Jerry, "what were you talking about at dinner? That I did?"

"Well," Mark admitted, "I thought, you know, after you helped with the chickens the other day, you came back and left the door open. Because they all got out, and they ate half of Emma's garden."

Bobby started to laugh, but Jerry stopped him. "I didn't," he said simply, so that Mark believed him.

"I'm sorry," said Mark. "And I thought you broke the egg on purpose, too."

"Well, I might have done that," Jerry agreed. "But I paid you back tonight."

"I guess you did." Mark looked at the bits of mud drying in Jerry's hair, and he felt better.

7

....

The rain stopped, and the river went down. A duck
family nested near the garden. The Swensons' cornfield withstood the flood better than most, because the
roots of so many weeds held the soil in place, and then
the corn grew and began to shade out the weeds. The
soybeans got planted, and Emma's tomatoes flowered.

Early July had always been the time to "walk the
beans." In the old days, Charlie said, they really
walked—all his father's children went out together, up
and down the long fields, to hand-pull the troublesome
weeds that herbicide did not kill. Cocklebur was the
worst, and sometimes ragweed or buttonweed. These

weeds germinated after the first application of herbicide, and if you didn't pull them they could grow up
and shade out the beans, which grew low to the
ground.

But nobody walked anymore. Now they would get
a bunch of kids together and put them on a row of
seats behind a tractor. Each kid would have a squirt
gun full of chemical. He or she was supposed to watch
the rows, one on either side, and squirt each weed as
the tractor went slowly by. It was still hot work, and
boring, and the chemicals stank. Afterward you had
to wash and wash and wash as if you were a bunch of
sprayed grapes from the store.

"Robert called about riding the beans," Addy said
one evening at supper. "He didn't know what we might
be planning to do this year."

"Am I old enough to go this year?" Jessica inter-
rupted.

"You're not allowed to bring paper and pencil," Mark
reminded her.

"Oh, shut up."

"Both of you be quiet a minute," Charlie scolded.
"What'd you tell him, Addy?"

"I said I'd speak with you about it. You know we
talked once about pulling by hand this year. I didn't
know what you think now, whether there are too many,
or what."

"It's a curious thing," Charlie said, sitting back. He grinned once, and then made himself look sober. "There was so much grass growing between the rows when I did the planting that the big weeds didn't get a chance to germinate. No herbicide at all, and we've never had so little cocklebur."

Addy didn't mind smiling at all. "You would do it again, wouldn't you?" she urged him. "You'd plant without chemicals. Even if you had extra money in the bank."

"I would at that."

"Well, I guess the four of us can pull by hand then, what there is. It'll go fast."

"Four?" asked Jessica hopefully. "Does that mean me, too?"

"That means you. And then we'll send the two of you over to Uncle Robert, to help him with his poor, weed-infested crop."

Mark knew that Jessica was looking forward to riding behind the tractor, thinking it would be fun. Little did she know.

It was stinking hot the morning they were set to begin. They all wore straw hats and took bottles of water and lemonade. The beanfields were not as big as the cornfields, but from the low seats behind the tractor, they seemed endless. And soon your back hurt from bending over to grab the rough weed stalks.

Jessica missed some, but Addy said it was all right, a few wouldn't matter.

After the first hour they took a break and traded places, Addy driving the tractor. "I have an idea," said Jessica. "We could let the chickens into the field. They're real good at pulling up plants."

Charlie laughed at her. "Just ask Mark."

They stopped work after half a day. Charlie said the kids nowadays were real candy fannies, but Addy said enough was enough, and the weeds would still be there tomorrow. In the end they worked for three half days, and Mark got to be the driver twice.

It was almost the middle of July when they went over to Uncle Robert's to ride for a day.

They were greeted by Silver, the Nelsons' cheerful three-legged dog, who had got run over by a truck a few years ago. He stayed a good distance from vehicles now, but he still treated children as if they were sheep, running around and around them in three-legged circles, barking encouragement.

"Hello, Silver. Good dog." Jessica stopped to pet him, but he almost pushed her past the storage bins, out toward the field. Following after, Mark understood why: There was a whole bunch of kids out there, and a good sheep dog likes his flock to stick together. He waved good-bye to his mother in the pickup, and walked over.

There were not only Bobby and Jerry, but Paul Johanssen and a couple of other kids from school, Aunt Sarah, and one of her cousins. And another person whom he had not expected, Emma Halvorsen. Mark waved at her, but did not get a chance to speak. Uncle Robert had taken the seed baskets off his twelve-row planter and replaced each with a homemade seat. Each rider was issued a short hand sprayer, connected by a plastic tube to the two thirty-gallon drums of herbicide that rode along with them. The work would go fast here.

Mark tried to get a seat beside Emma, but he ended up between Bobby and Jerry instead. Even so, he was feeling pretty good about life. The chickens were laying really well, and the first tomatoes were getting ripe in the garden. "I see you got kind of a big ditch opening up over there," he remarked as the tractor started into one side of the field. "That happen in the big rain?"

"Yup." Bobby squirted the first weed, reminding Mark to pay attention. *Pssht. Pssht.* All up and down the row, people began aiming their guns, and the old remembered chemical smell filled Mark's nose.

" 'Course we didn't have any of that kind of erosion problem in our fields," Mark said loudly. "The weeds hold the soil in place, in a big rain."

"Good idea, if you want to raise weeds," Bobby sneered.

"You seem to have quite a few weeds right here," Mark replied.

"We wouldn't have so many if you watched what you're doing," Jerry yelled. Mark did feel guilty for a moment; a big giant ragweed had just slipped right by him. "A few don't matter," he said, quoting his mother.

"Yeah, that's the Swenson policy," said Bobby. "That the way Emma and you run the garden, too? Excuse me, Mr. Weed, don't let me get in your way." He did a phony little bow off the side of the planter.

"Bobby Nelson, you stay in your seat," Aunt Sarah called out from a couple of seats down the row. "We don't need anyone falling off the tractor. Robert!" She yelled forward at her husband, trying to get him to hear over the tractor noise. "Robert! Not so fast! Slow down!" She gestured to him, but he just shrugged and kept going about the same.

Bobby sat straight, but he grinned over at Mark in a nasty way. They rode quietly for a few minutes, squirting busily, until Bobby leaned across and said to Jerry, "Why did the chicken cross the road?"

"Because he wanted to get to Mark's house," Jerry answered promptly.

Mark didn't even answer. What a dumb joke.

The day began to get hot again. They stopped for a break so everyone could have something to drink. Mark figured he would snatch a seat beside Emma this

94

time, but then he noticed that all the girls were sitting at one end, and boys at the other. Aunt Sarah, who was right in the middle, began remarking on it and laughing. "Oh, these children," she said to her cousin. "Look how they split up, aren't they something?"

"But you know what will happen in a few years!" her cousin replied with a wink.

So Mark went back to his old seat. But apparently Jerry had noticed his hesitation.

"You wanted to sit by Emma, *didn't* you?"

"No."

"You and Emma really go for each other, don't you?"

"No. And anyway, it's none of your business, so just shut up."

"Too bad she's so ugly."

"Yeah," Bobby chimed in, "too bad she needs braces."

"You just missed another buttonweed," Jerry pointed out.

Mark flung his gun around in anger. Without meaning to, he squeezed the trigger—it must have been just his fist closing up, without his thinking about it. However it was, a stream of chemical shot out over Bobby's head. Bobby yelled as if he'd been murdered, pulled his own gun upward, and shot back—aiming at Mark, he shot high, so the chemical flew over Mark's head toward the girls' end of the planter. Now there were shrieks from everywhere, with Aunt Sarah loudest of all. The tractor stopped. Mark and Bobby gave each other one level look of hatred and guilt—now they had really messed up.

Jessica was still screaming. Uncle Robert had climbed down from the tractor, and Aunt Sarah's cousin was lifting Jessica down as if she were sick. Mark looked over at Emma, who was shouting, "Who did that? Who would do such a stupid thing? What's the matter with you guys?"

"It was Bobby!" Mark hopped down, furious. "Bobby shot chemical at everybody!"

"Jessica got some!" another voice yelled. "It's all over her arm."

"Someone better wash her off fast," said Emma, glowering at Bobby.

"He shot me first! You stupid jerk! What'd you shoot me for?" Bobby raised his arm at Mark again.

"Look, her arm's getting red already." Aunt Sarah and Uncle Robert together started to lead Jessica away from the fighting children. Mark raised his chemical gun to defend himself. Bobby jumped forward, shaking his own metal wand, and Mark felt for his trigger again.

"You better watch it," he warned. Without taking his eye off Bobby's weapon, he realized that the other kids had formed a frozen circle around them, watching.

He wondered what the chemical *would* do; he wondered what it was doing now, to Jessica. But he would not back down to Bobby Nelson.

"Look out!" yelled Jerry.

There was a streak of movement, and then Emma was standing between them. "Stop it," she said, very seriously.

Ashamed, but still wary, Mark lowered his wand a couple of inches. Bobby did not move.

"Put it down, Bobby," said a voice from the circle.

"Tell her to get out of there," was his answer.

Emma glared at Bobby, but he would not meet her eyes. Suddenly she knocked at his wand hard with her fist. In his surprise he yelped, letting it fall harmlessly to the ground. With his other hand, he socked Emma in the shoulder, but she slapped him right back in the face, hard. For a few seconds, he just stood there, surprised.

Then one of the kids cheered, while another one began to laugh. Mark had an awful feeling that Bobby was going to start fighting Emma in earnest, and if he did, Mark was going to have to fight, too. But to his immense relief, Uncle Robert appeared and took control. He sent Mark and Emma with Aunt Sarah to run to the house with Jessica to wash her, and he told them not to come back today. Mark heard him yelling at Bobby and Jerry as he left the field.

Aunt Sarah stripped off Jessica's shirt and washed her at the outside hose before taking her inside for hot water and soap. Then Emma turned to Mark, to ask him how it got started.

"Bobby Nelson shot my sister with herbicide."

"I know. But before that."

"They were being obnoxious. They kept picking on me. I hate them."

"Yeah, but why were they doing that?" Emma was so persistent that Mark almost didn't like her for a moment.

"How should I know why?" Then he remembered. He guessed he had to tell Emma everything. "I shot some stuff first. But only by accident, and it just went off to the side. They were making me mad, making fun of our corn."

Emma didn't say anything more. She began to walk toward the barns, so Mark followed her. There were the steers, their silly big ears stuck out to the side. You could tell which was Bobby's by how clean it was. "I'm surprised he doesn't put bows in its hair," Mark mumbled.

Emma smiled. "Do you think Jessica will be all right?"

"She better be." He made a fist. "Or I'll kill that guy."

"No, you won't."

"You were almost ready to kill him."

Emma thought about that. "Well, I guess I would have punched him out if he had tried to shoot any more chemicals around."

"See what I mean?" Coming back to the house, Mark saw Jessica and Aunt Sarah emerge. Jessica was wearing a clean boy's shirt. Her upper arm had developed a red rash, but Aunt Sarah said she thought it would be all right, although she had called Addy to come and take her to the doctor.

"So that was my Bobby, eh?" she asked Mark sadly.

Mark squirmed uncomfortably. Emma was still listening, so now he had to tell the whole thing. "Well, we kind of got into a fight. I guess I kind of shot first. Only I didn't mean to, it was just an accident."

"Well, we can't afford that kind of accident when we're working with chemicals," she said severely. "I'm going to make the boys pay this doctor's bill, and I think your parents may ask you to chip in as well."

Mark nodded. It was fair.

In another minute his mother was there. She took all three of them, so Mark and Emma had to wait around at the doctor's office. It was a bad-smelling place that gave Mark depressing thoughts, and even made him realize that he had started out the day by not being very nice to his cousins.

Jessica was sucking a lollipop when she finally came

out. Addy looked a bit more relaxed, too, because the doctor thought that probably nothing worse than a rash would come of it, though they were lucky. He had praised them for washing her so quickly and thoroughly.

Addy was more understanding than Mark had hoped, when she got him alone. "Still," she said seriously, "it doesn't do any good to hit people, or try to get back at them. It always comes back around to you in the end."

Mark wanted to say that his father had pretty nearly punched out Uncle Robert, but he decided he'd better not. Pretty nearly was not the same as doing it.

When they had all gotten home and Mark had tended the chickens, he felt better. He counted up the money from the eggs sold this week and gave it to his mother to keep. Jessica went up to her room to write up her brush with death, as she called it, while Addy went back to sewing on the quilt. She had piles of little bars of cloth, mostly browns and greens, some with tiny patterns on them, which she was sewing together on the machine. Mark asked her to show him how the pattern would look.

She showed him a square that was all sewn together. She said it was called Log Cabin.

"Looks more like farm fields," he said. "When there are different crops. All the different colors, brown and green, side by side."

She laughed. "So it does. Maybe I did it because of looking at the fields all day, without even knowing it."

"Maybe you could win a prize at the fair with your quilt."

"I doubt it. Those prize quilts are all sewn by hand." She gave Mark a significant look. "Prizes aren't that important to me. I don't need to be a better quilter than someone else. I'm just doing this because it's fun, and the quilt will be useful." The sewing machine whirred again, and Mark felt sad, knowing what she meant.

"You don't think I'm going to win, do you? I mean me and Emma. You don't think we're going to beat Bobby and Jerry."

"No, I don't. Those cows will go for a thousand dollars, and all you kids will have is a pile of tomatoes and more eggs than the neighborhood wants. I don't say that to make you feel bad. I think you have both done really great, working together, and finding projects that don't cost too much at the start. After all, Dad had the same problem. He won't beat out anyone at profits this year. But he'll make enough to keep the farm, and that's what he cares about."

She was right, but still Mark felt sad, thinking of the hundred-dollar prize that Eric would be giving to Bobby or Jerry. He hoped at least that some other calf raiser would beat them out.

8
■■■■■■

By the end of July, the corn was as tall as a man, even in the Swenson fields. It had grown fast enough to shade out most of the weeds, and fast enough to make Mr. Swenson talk more enthusiastically about his "experiment" when Mark followed him into the Eat Shop. When he went to reserve his space at the grain elevator, he joked happily with the manager about how large a crop he was expecting.

"That's good, Charlie," the man replied. "Some of the farmers lost quite a bit, during the heavy rains. That time the river flooded, over toward your place."

"We did all right that night, didn't even lose a chicken."

The crops in Emma's garden began to ripen. First there were a few carrots and tomatoes, which they gave to their families. And then everything seemed to get ripe all at once. One hot, hot day, when the chickens were loitering in the shade, Mark and Emma began picking tomatoes and beans in earnest. The tomatoes were hard work, because each one had to be handled carefully, so it wouldn't get squashed. They set the tomatoes in lettuce crates, which Emma's mother had begged from the grocery store, and when they ran out they set them in laundry baskets. But the crates soon got too heavy, so they had to take little bags down the row, and walk back frequently, lifting each tomato twice.

But that wasn't as bad as the beans, which grew low to the ground, and had to be picked one by one. The beans could go into paper grocery bags, but there were so terribly many of them. Mark's hands got sore. He and Emma sent Lisa and Jessica back and forth for lemonade or more bags and baskets, but after a few trips Lisa stumbled over a hoe, spilled the lemonade onto the bags, and cried. Emma took the little girls back to the house, saying it was too hot for them. Mark thought it was too hot for him, too, but he didn't say so.

The next day was market day. Fortunately it was a little cooler, and Emma's mother found an old beach umbrella in the attic, so they could sit under some shade. They had the first few bunches of cornflowers, and when they were all set up, with the green umbrella, the blue flowers, the red tomatoes, and twenty dozen brown eggs, everything looked very nice, Mark thought. Anyway, it was better than picking.

At least at first. When the car drove away and left them sitting there in the empty lot at the end of town, Mark suddenly realized he should have brought something to do. Emma had a book to read, but he had nothing.

He watched the cars and pickups coming into town. He watched who went into the Eat Shop, and the hardware store. He smiled as cars drove past them, the drivers sometimes waving in recognition. "Say, you kids look real cute there." Then the car would pass on down the street and stop in front of the grocery store.

Finally an older woman who lived just beyond their stand stopped and bought three tomatoes for seventy-five cents. She said the produce looked very nice, and she asked Emma what book she was reading. Then she was gone.

Restlessly Mark got up and paced around. He was annoyed with Emma for just sitting there, lost in some fantasy world of her book. She wasn't paying attention; she didn't see that it wasn't working. At this rate they might earn two dollars for a whole day, and all their weeks of hard work could turn into a bushel of sun-cooked tomatoes. He thought about 4-H, about coming in to report so little profit, and the Nelsons' steers getting bigger all the time.

And he remembered Eric talking about marketing.

"Emma, I'm going to make a sign. Give me the change box." They had brought twenty dollars in coins and dollar bills, for making change.

She looked up dimly, her mind far away. "We need the change."

"Not at this rate. Here, give it." He took five dollars of the money and walked down to the variety store, where he bought three pieces of posterboard and a set of colored markers. He brought them back to the shade of the umbrella, and began to write. TOMATOES, he wrote, in purple. ONLY $.25, in red.

"Hey, that's a good idea." Emma dropped her book face down and took a piece of posterboard. In blue, she drew a pretty good cornflower, and then made green leaves. "How much are we charging for the flowers?"

Mark shrugged. "How much does the man with the truck charge?"

"His sign said a dollar a flower, but those were big ones. How about a dollar for a bunch?"

"Okay, but we only have six bunches."

"That's all right. If we just get some customers up

here, then they might buy the other stuff. Even if we run out of flowers."

"Good idea." He wrote down all their items on his own poster: BEANS, $1.50 PER BAG. FRESH DELICIOUS FARM EGGS, $.90/DOZEN. Then he wrote SOLD BY MARK SWENSON AND EMMA HALVORSEN, CORNER OF MAIN AND HARTLAND. Emma made a beautiful border with more flowers and sunshine and smily faces. Mark went down and stood one poster up in the lip of the big window in the grocery store, right by the door where people would see it going in. Then he put Emma's sign up in the window of the post office, on the other side of the street.

As soon as he got back, he looked down the street and saw a woman start into the grocery store, look at the sign, turn and wave at the children. She hesitated, and walked up the block to them. She was one of the women who worked in the library at school.

"Well, aren't you kids something? And Emma's got her book, I see. Good for you, Emma, not wasting time. You don't want to put it down like that, sweetheart, you'll break the binding. These beans look very nice, are they quite fresh?"

Mark told her they were picked yesterday. "Well, aren't you something. I never did get my vegetable garden going this spring, what with all the rain. I'll have a bag of those beans. And half a dozen tomatoes. My, look at those nice brown eggs. I heard you were selling eggs, Mark. I believe I'll just take a dozen. And what do I owe you?"

Emma added it up. Six tomatoes at twenty-five cents made a dollar fifty. Plus a dollar fifty for the beans made three dollars. Plus ninety cents for eggs made three ninety. The library lady handed them a five-dollar bill. Mark dug the change out of his pocket and gave her a dollar ten, and put the five in the change box. And just as she walked away, here came someone else.

More customers came. Mrs. Swenson dropped by to see how they were doing, and bought beans and tomatoes herself. They ran out of coins, but Emma ran down to the bank to change another twenty, and then three of the bank workers came up at lunchtime to buy. They ran out of flowers first, and then eggs. And suddenly, Mr. Penny, who owned the grocery store, was standing right in front of them, with their sign in his hand. He was not smiling.

"I don't remember giving permission to have this poster in my window."

Mark felt Emma look at him, as if he was supposed to have asked. "I just, I didn't know, I've seen lots of signs there, I'm sorry. . . ."

Mr. Penny dropped the posterboard on the ground. "I give permission to some advertisers. But that's my window, and I pay taxes on it, and I'd as soon not have your sign. I have my own produce to sell. You kids think you can do what you want because you're kids, but you can't leave your junk all over private property."

Mark and Emma both waited submissively, not sure what to do. "I'm sorry, Mr. Penny," Emma said softly. Mark just wanted him to go away, and he did, stepping on the poster as he went.

"The crochety old geezer," said Emma. "He's always like that. He follows kids around his store, thinking they'll steal his candy. I hate the jerk."

Mark agreed. "I never talked to him before. And I hope I never do again."

"We can't really be taking that much business away from him."

Mark shrugged. "What if we are? Who cares?"

"But what are we going to do about advertising?"

It was clear that the sign in the grocery store window was doing them more good than anything else. There was a lamppost near the store, and Mark wondered aloud about fastening a sign to that. "Before we do this again, I'll make a better sign. I'll paint it, on a piece of wood."

But it was Emma who came up with the best idea. The next day she made a sandwich board, two poster-boards connected by strings, that you could hang over your shoulders. Mark said he didn't actually want to walk around town with that on, but Emma suggested that Jessica could do it. "She's always wanting to get published. This way she'll be a walking publication herself. Maybe the paper will print a story about her."

"She might go for it. Especially if we let her write the poster. In poetry."

They had another picking day, and the first of the corn was ripe, so they added corn to their price list, at two dollars a dozen. And Mark brought a bigger supply of eggs. Then they spent three seventy-five on lemonade and paper cups, thinking people might come for refreshments. Emma said they should give the lemonade away free. She said it was called a "come-on." But Mark wanted to charge at least a dime. In the end they drank most of it themselves, so the lemonade turned out not to be a good money-maker. The rest of the stuff did fine. Jessica spent an hour in the morning and another in the afternoon walking around in the posterboards, which said:

MARK AND EMMA SELL THE BEST
VEGETABLES AND EGGS WITH ZEST

And on the back side it said:

SUPPORT YOUR 4-H CITIZENS
BUY YOUR EGGS FROM MARK'S HENS

NO MORE SHOPPING DILEMMA
BUY YOUR VEGETABLES FROM EMMA

109

In three days of selling, they brought in $168.50. Then they had to subtract the lemonade, the poster-board, and the markers, so that brought the income down to $157. So far, their total profit was $169.25.

"Net," Emma reminded Mark proudly. They had long since paid off his mother for the feed and her father for the tilling. The note was gone from the Swensons' refrigerator door.

They felt very good going into the next 4-H meeting, knowing that neither the Nelsons nor anyone else had any income at all yet. But they were in for some so-bering news. One of the boys who was raising a sheep had found a woman who did home spinning and she had bought his wool for $25. And he still had the sheep to sell for meat.

The Nelson boys, as usual, had the biggest steers. Bobby figured his profit was going to be $287, at the current price for beef, if his steer reached eight hundred pounds.

Emma whispered that they still had plenty of time to make another $120, but Mark wasn't so sure. The hens were laying less now, and he had lost several regular customers, who said they had more eggs than they could use. Their last trip to town had netted less money. The beans were getting old and people didn't want them. They weren't doing too well on corn, because most people had patches of their own, and the only real crop left to come was watermelon. But there weren't as many of them as they had hoped. Bugs had eaten some of the plants pretty badly, after the chickens had gotten through with them. And Mark had to get more chicken feed.

"Besides," he told Emma, "Bobby isn't telling the whole truth. His steer will probably weigh more than eight hundred. He's saving that for a surprise. Last year his was over nine hundred."

That made Emma look less happy. For Bobby to make an extra hundred dollars, all he had to do was wait for the steer to gain more weight. For them, it was hours in the hot garden picking, and hours waiting around town for customers, one at a time.

Jerry was whispering to kids to watch out for Emma, she was likely to bash you one, but neither Mark nor Emma spoke to him at all.

Addy was supposed to pick Mark up after the 4-H meeting, but she was late, which gave Mark an opportunity to talk to Mr. Fogelman while they folded the chairs. "I was wondering," Mark began.

"Yes?"

"Do you think a person can get a good crop without using chemicals?"

Eric answered seriously. "It's no piece of cake, diversifying and changing. It's definitely more work.

And more risk. But if your dad keeps on the way he's going, some duck somewhere is going to have healthier babies."

"At first I was embarrassed at how weedy the fields were," Mark volunteered. "But now, at least something is growing. I don't know. It's better than losing the farm."

"Well," said Eric, "I'm real pleased with the experiments you and Emma are making. That was exactly what I was hoping for. Of course, an experiment doesn't always win prizes, the first time around."

Mark understood what he was saying—that Bobby and Jerry were still going to have bigger profits, and one of them would win the $100. He nodded, but sadly. "I think I hear my mom."

"All right then. Take care, and mind the chickens."

9

∎∎∎∎∎∎∎

Mark's mother was writing a story for the paper about some citizens who wanted to restore the old movie theater. Mark bothered her while she wrote. "Did you finish the quilt?"

"Almost." Her fingers kept on working at the computer keys.

"You could get a piece of blue material and make a river going across it."

"Uh-huh."

"Eric says he used to love the river."

No answer.

"Emma and I saw ducks. One day after picking we

went down to the river and saw a whole family of ducks."

"Did you?" She didn't look up.

"Eric says we're not going to win his prize."

She looked up.

"You know, the prize he offered for the most profit."

"He told you that?"

"Well, not in so many words. But that's what he was saying."

"Is Bobby winning?"

"Of course, Mom. Bobby wins everything. But that's not the most important thing."

"How close is it?"

Mark showed her his and Emma's balance sheet, and then he told her about Bobby's, as closely as he could remember. She switched the computer off, getting up from the desk and crossing to the kitchen to look out the window.

"A hundred and twenty dollars. That's not so much. How many eggs are left?"

"Well, they don't lay quite as well when it's hot. But we've got fifteen dozen in the refrigerator."

"Fifteen dollars, more or less. How many tomatoes are left?"

"Oh, bushels. But most people have them in their own gardens now."

"What else?"

Mark couldn't believe this. Here she was, adding it all up in her head, after all she'd said to him. "There's still some corn. And the watermelon."

"And my quilt. I could stay up and finish it tonight."

"What?"

But she didn't even answer him. She got out the big Twin Cities phone book, and began looking for something. She looked as determined as the day she had driven the Steiger. Mark looked over her shoulder at the number she picked out—Minneapolis Farmers Market, Information for Sellers.

Leaving her index finger on the number, she looked at Mark and said, "You don't have to lie down and lose. Just because everyone says you're going to. If I drive you to Minneapolis on Saturday, will you and Emma get up at three in the morning, and sell all day?"

"Oh, you bet we will!"

That Friday was the biggest picking day of all. They picked every tomato, even if it was still green. They kept finding more watermelons hidden under the broad leaves, until they had picked fifty-eight of them. They harvested two bushels of corn, and twelve dozen cornflowers, which they packaged together with rubber bands in bunches of six. They looked at the beans, but they were too overgrown, hard, or yellow; they looked at the last carrots, but they were like wooden sticks.

So they loaded their produce into the pickup. Emma slept over, in Jessica's room, and when it was still dark they got up and loaded in twenty-five dozen eggs and the quilt.

Emma couldn't believe that Addy wanted to sell the quilt, but Addy said she could probably get $150 for it, and she could always make another. Of course, that wouldn't be part of their 4-H project. But it would make their stall look nice.

The drive took two hours, during which Mark slept, until he felt the car stop at the first traffic light of the city. They passed the shopping mall where they went once a year for school clothes, whizzed around on city highways that made Addy nervous, and crossed the Mississippi River, which runs right through the city. It was still early, and birds were singing, and the buildings and streets looked rosy with beautiful light.

Emma read the map, to help find the place. The market was loud and confusing. They parked next to a huge semi, with men unloading crates from the back, calling out orders and jokes to one another that Mark could not understand. They looked surprised to see Addy, and smiled at the pickup, which looked like a dwarf there. One of the men tipped his cap. "Mornin', ma'am."

She told the children to stay with the truck while she went to sign in with a manager. She came back looking less confused, with a piece of paper and a map of the market, with an X showing where they would sell their produce. They had to carry the bushel baskets down a long corridor. Mark and Emma each took one side. They made several trips, and when all their produce was carried, Addy said it was time to look for a cup of coffee. "The market won't open for another half hour. I wonder if we can just leave everything here."

Mark offered to stand guard. He couldn't bear to have stuff stolen now. "Bring me something," he said.

They brought him a can of pop, just as the first customers began strolling through the market. On one side of them was a man selling every kind of produce— not only corn and tomatoes, but beans and peppers, lettuce and carrots, even spinach and peas. Where did he get all that, this time of year? On the other side was a stall that specialized in tomatoes: cherry tomatoes, plum tomatoes, yellow tomatoes, and big fresh bunches of strong-smelling basil.

Mark looked at their bushel baskets. "We should make this look better," he said. "Too bad we don't have Jessica with the sandwich board."

They hung the quilt at the back of the stall, like a backdrop. They arranged the flowers at the front, and they set out a few of the egg cartons open, so you could see the pretty, light brown color of the eggs. They set just a few of their best-looking tomatoes and water-melons in view, and put up their price list. Mark went out front to check. They were charging a little bit less for tomatoes than their neighbor, but then, they didn't have such fancy varieties.

The day started just like on the corner of Main and Hartland—nobody stopped. Mark and Emma went for a stroll around, looking at the things for sale, and the people. There was honey, and mounds of tomatoes and corn everywhere, and flowers, much fancier flowers—roses and carnations, irises and gladiolus. There were eggs, fresh bread and pies, berries, and a stall that sold fish. Their own stall seemed now to have nothing special about it, and Mark felt discouraged. He saw an old man in stained clothing just standing in a corner, smoking a cigarette, and then coughing and coughing, as if he should be with a doctor. It made Mark feel sad and lonely. "Let's go back," he suggested.

As they rounded the corner, someone was stopped at their stall. It was a woman, asking questions about the quilt. But when she was done, she went away without buying anything. She stopped and bought basil and tomatoes next door.

Then a bright voice said, "Oh, brown eggs. How much?"

"A dollar a dozen," Mark said, wondering why she couldn't read the sign.

"One dozen then. Thank you very much."

The hours went slowly, but bit by bit, they sold a little of this, and a little of that. There was only one stool, so they had to take turns sitting on it. Addy had brought a book about how to write advertisements, so she wasn't much company. Emma seemed tired. Around noon, just after they had eaten their sandwiches, the tomato and basil stall closed up. Emma went to talk to the woman, who said she always sold eighty percent by noon, and the rest wasn't worth it. But business picked up for them, with the tomato competition gone. City workers came in on their lunch breaks. Now they all got to their feet and sold together, and Mark learned to say encouraging things. "We grew these vegetables ourselves, part of a 4-H project." "The chickens are mine, they have an outside yard to scratch in and they're real happy." "I just turned twelve, yes, ma'am." "No, she's not my sister, she's my friend." "It sure was a lot of work, but we didn't drop any of them." People were more likely to buy when you talked to them. And suddenly, looking around, there was only one bushel of tomatoes left, and half a dozen melons, and the quilt.

Then an older lady stopped, with her hair in curls, and three different rings on each hand. She was marching past, *tromp, tromp, tromp,* as if she had an airplane to catch, when she stopped short, eyes on the quilt.

She seemed disappointed when she heard that Addy had done the work on a machine. But still she didn't leave. "How much do you want for it?"

Mark saw Addy hesitate. He looked around, at their nearly empty stall and the stuffed cash box. He heard her say, "Three hundred fifty."

"But it's only a machine quilt!" the woman exclaimed. "You'll never get that for it."

Addy just looked at her, and she marched off, *tromp, tromp, tromp.* Suddenly she wheeled back. "I need a bushel of tomatoes for canning. What variety are these?"

"Big Boys," said Emma.

"Oh, that'll do, I suppose. Most of the other stalls have closed up. I'm a little late. How much for a whole bushel? You're not going to charge me the regular per pound price."

The children glanced at Addy, who replied swiftly, "Twenty dollars."

"How about fifteen?"

Addy looked tired. "Seventeen."

"Fine. Have your boy there carry it to my car." She gave Addy a twenty-dollar bill, and Addy pushed the last basket toward Mark. He struggled to lift it, and then said, "Come on, Emma."

It seemed like half a mile to the woman's car, which was a dark red Mercedes. Emma laughed on the way back. "You wouldn't think someone who drives a Mercedes would can their own tomatoes."

"And haggle the most over the prices."

Now there was nothing more to do than load the empty baskets into the truck, along with the last few watermelons and two dozen eggs, and the quilt. On the way home, the children held the cash box in their laps and counted the money together. They had a hundred and thirty-nine dollars!

"How come you asked so much for the quilt?" asked Mark.

Addy thought. "I guess I didn't want to sell it," she replied. "Not to her."

"I'm glad," Mark said. "Let's keep it. Anyway, we have a hundred and thirty-nine dollars."

"But don't forget," said Emma, "we brought twenty dollars in change."

"Oh, yeah. Okay, so we made a hundred and nine-teen."

"Minus the gas," Addy put in. "You'll owe me about fifteen for gas."

"All right. A hundred and four."

"Plus," said Addy, "there's tax."

"Tax!" Both children looked at her, almost angry.

"That's the way it goes," said Addy. "The city charges two percent on everything sold at the market. Now who can figure that out in your head?"

"I can figure out that it's not fair," Mark complained.

"Oh, yes it is," said Addy. "The city built the stalls and paved the streets. They provide the electric lights, advertising for the market, and a manager to run it."

"And a policeman to guard it," said Emma. "I saw him."

"Do you think the city has shelters for the homeless?" asked Mark.

"Certainly. They do the best they can."

"All right then. Two percent of a hundred and . . ." But he had to get a paper and pencil. The tax came to $2.38, giving them a final profit of $101.62. "It might be enough to beat Bobby," he said.

"Next year," said Emma sleepily, "I'm going to grow basil."

10
·······

It was a wonderful smell, just like his daydream—a mixture of popcorn, manure, diesel fuel, sawdust, and a shampoo fragrance from Emma's hair as she sat beside him on the bleachers, watching the cattle judging. But of course it was not Mark who was leading a large steer around the ring by a rope halter. There was a circle of a dozen kids, all with good-looking animals, but Mark was not one of them. Bobby was one, and Jerry was one.

He tried not to mind. His father was sitting beside Uncle Robert, not quarreling now, and on the other side his mother sat with Emma's mother, chattering away and not paying attention. Beside them, Lisa watched with big eyes while Jessica took notes. Across the way he could see Eric sitting by Paul, who had done very well with his pig, but had nearly cried when it was time to take him to the packing house. Paul was not used to raising animals to eat.

The children showing their cattle were dismissed from the ring. That was the first round. The audience waited, and in a few minutes names were read out for the second round. Only four 4-H-ers were asked to return: Martha Wilson, Randy Sutter, Robert Nelson, Gerald Nelson.

Emma made a face at Mark.

Each animal was led once around the ring, all by itself. The judges knew what it weighed, but they looked at how the weight was distributed: how much in the shoulders, the hind legs, the steak areas around the ribs. They judged the animal's health by the quality of the hair, which the Nelsons had combed and cleaned until it shone. And they also judged the owner on showmanship: how well he or she handled the animal, whether he or she could make it go and stop, or stand at attention in front of the judges' bench.

Randy's animal suddenly kicked and jerked free of its rope. It ran along the side of the round pen, looking for a door. A man who worked for the fair caught hold of the dragging rope and brought the steer back under control. Randy flushed with frustration.

Bobby's steer had the biggest shoulders, Mark showed Emma. But Martha's stood in exactly the right pose; she had excellent control.

"What does it matter," Emma asked, "when you're just going to eat it?"

Mark shrugged. "That's the way 4-H does it."

The animals were led away, and there was another pause. "Can we go now?" Lisa asked her mother.

"No, honey, we have to wait. Just a little longer."

The animals would be slaughtered the day after the showing was over, and the judges would also inspect the meat. The best cuts of meat were supposed to be well marbled with fat, but Eric had said that times were changing. More people wanted leaner beef, or even other types of meat that have less cholesterol. But good fat beef still brought an excellent price. And on Thursday, the day after the meat inspection, 4-H would have its final meeting of the year. And Bobby and Jerry and all the other kids would know their exact income.

The loudspeaker crackled. "Gerald Nelson." Jerry came in all by himself, led his steer once around the ring, and got a yellow ribbon for third place.

"Martha Wilson." Mark groaned. That meant Bobby was first, as usual. He watched Martha's parents taking her picture as the red ribbon was tied to the rope.

And then it was Bobby's turn. The audience clapped for him, and a woman from the big county newspaper snapped his picture, as did Aunt Sarah.

Uncle Robert got very cheerful. He leaned forward and called down the bleachers to Mark. "You enter your chickens, Mark? They have a pretty good poultry competition, I understand."

"No, I didn't."

"Didn't even enter them?"

"No, I didn't, Uncle Robert."

"Emma enter anything?"

"I was going to enter my flowers, but I sold them all," she answered.

"Oh, I see." He turned to his wife. "Well, Sarah, the boys did it again. Let's go congratulate them."

Mark's own parents went to join the crowd around the winners, too. Even Mr. Fogelman was shaking their hands. "C'mon, Emma," said Mark, "let's split."

Thursday arrived. The kids who came to 4-H each had their balance sheets ready. Mark and Emma had made separate final accounts, but they each wrote at the top "Cob Town Rural Co-Op," and they paper-clipped their sheets together. Mark had sold another fifteen dozen eggs since the Twin Cities trip, giving him a total of $132.35. Emma's garden total was $150.52, for a grand total of $282.87.

Eric talked to them all about making final adjustments, but Mark knew his sheet was perfect. Then Eric collected all the sheets himself, and said he would study them over. He gave the kids a recess.

Bobby wouldn't tell what his profit was. Paul Johanssen said he made about $120, which really wasn't bad for a town kid. A couple of people had actually lost money, including the boy who had sold the wool for his sheep, because at the last minute he decided not to sell the sheep. He had given it a name and everything.

"How much you make from your flowers?" Jerry asked Emma with a sneer. "You make twenty dollars?"

"You'll find out," she said.

But Mark's heart was in his mouth when they went back in. What would they find out?

Eric made the announcement right away: The greatest profit was made by Jerry Nelson, who deserved everyone's congratulations. He passed the sheets back.

Mark felt ready to give up farming. All the hours of work, all the sweat, all the flies and mosquitoes he had endured, the night he saved the chickens from the flood, everything seemed lost, all for nothing. He knew he shouldn't think that way. Winning isn't everything. They had still made a good profit; looking at the sheets as Eric returned them, he saw that Jerry had made only $19 more.

He stared at his and Emma's sheets again. And then

he realized their mistake. "Wait a minute!" he shouted.

They were all quiet, looking at him. "Emma and I both subtracted some of the same expenses! Look here. She took off for the gas, I took off for the gas. She took off for the advertising, I took off for the advertising. We both even put down the taxes in the Cities. That's not right, we only paid that once."

"I see." Eric held out his hand for the papers, and looked them over, nodding his head. "Yes, he's right, I think we have an error here. Let's just take this calculator and refigure."

But as soon as his finger hit the first number, Jerry jumped up. "That's no fair! There's two of them! You can't count both together. No fair. If they count together, then me and Bobby count together."

Eric looked up, listening. For once, Mark wished Eric hadn't been such a good listener. He had his hand on his chin, while Bobby chimed in, "Yeah, right. Each one on his own, isn't that right?"

Eric looked at Emma. "We agreed from the beginning," she said. "Mark and I. We were partners. He worked in the garden, a whole lot. And his mother drove us to the Cities together. And he would never have bought the chickens if it hadn't been for Lisa. And his sister Jessica wrote the advertising."

"That's right," Mark agreed. "We said we were together from the beginning. Nobody complained about it then."

"No fair," said Jerry.

"I think," said Eric, "we will have to allow them the co-op, since we did accept the idea at the beginning. And they did work together, a great deal. Jerry, did you feed and train Bobby's steer, at all?"

Jerry looked surprised. "Not me. He feeds his own."

"All right then, that's settled. Now, what is the final figure?" He tapped at the calculator. Gasoline, $15. Advertising, $4.75. Tax, $2.38. Then he added the amount deducted twice, $22.13, to the final net profit, Emma's $150.52, plus Mark's $132.35.

And there it was, on the calculator—$305 even, just $3.10 over Jerry's net profit. They had won.

Eric looked very happy, Mark thought, as he shook their hands, and gave them the check for the hundred dollars. "Have one of your parents cash it," he said, "and then you can split it."

Then he gave everybody a lecture about the meaning of this experience, but Mark didn't care too much. He had won the prize, and Bobby and Jerry were both surprised and angry, and he was glad. And Emma was still his partner, and he still had the chickens, while they had to start all over again. And he had a pile of chicken manure that Mr. Halvorsen had promised to till into the garden for next year, as soon as he had a chance.

COB TOWNERS WIN PRIZE, read Jessica's headline that night. Addy said this story would really get into the paper, though she thought Cindy might edit it some. Mark hadn't realized that his own sister could be so proud of him.

The next morning, Charlie Swenson cashed the check, with Mark and Emma standing right there, so they each had five crisp ten-dollar bills in their hands. Mark asked Emma to spend the rest of the day at the fair with him. "It's the last day," he reminded her.

"Sure," she said. "I was going to ask you. My mom said I can stay all day, and she'll pick us up tonight. They're coming for the tractor pulls. And I don't even have to watch Lisa."

"Why don't you let me hold on to some of that money," said Mr. Swenson. "You've been good loan customers, so now you can make a deposit with me. You each keep ten dollars for now, and I'll keep the rest safe."

Somewhat reluctantly, Mark gave back four of the bills, and Emma did the same. His father left them at the fair grounds with a wave. The first thing they did was buy two raffle tickets for a brand new International Harvester tractor, for a dollar a ticket. Then they bought hot dogs and popcorn, and they rode on the Tilt-a-Whirl and lost at three different shooting games. For a while they watched the Time Shaft, which neither of them had ever been on before, until they decided to try it. At least Mark did—he had to coax Emma to come with him.

"I didn't know you would ever be afraid of anything," he said to her.

"You wait," she promised. "You'll be afraid."

And he was. The Time Shaft was round and you stood against the wall. It turned faster and faster until you were pressed against the wall, and then the floor began to drop out from under your feet and you were just hanging there, like a picture without a nail. But the worst part was that you couldn't even scream because your cheeks were pushed back against your teeth.

At last they slowed, and the floor came back up. Mark's legs shook, and Emma looked pale under her summer tan. "That was great," he said faintly as they walked off.

She rolled her eyes at him, but she took his hand and kept holding it as they strolled away.

SUSAN SHARPE researched *Chicken Bucks,* her third novel, on Minnesota and Iowa farms, where she "met children and animals, rode on tractors, and talked to farmers in the evenings." She adds, "It was an usually wet spring, a fact that worked its way into my story."

Like *Chicken Bucks,* Ms. Sharpe's previous books feature environmental concerns. *Waterman's Boy,* an *American Bookseller* "Pick of the Lists," is "a well-paced ecological mystery–adventure" *(Booklist).* In *Spirit Quest* she "brings to a stark, realistic climax the clashes between ancient and modern, Indian and white, natural and man-made. . . . the book's bold, original subject matter shines brilliantly" *(Publishers Weekly).*

A teacher of writing and children's literature, Ms. Sharpe lives with her family in Arlington, Virginia.